Praise for
SONG OF THE HEART

In *Song of the Heart*, Janet Litherland has crafted a page-turner brimming with romance and suspense. Susan finds true love with Rhys during her brief sojourn in Wales, unaware that both are destined to hurdle personal trials that will keep them apart for many years. While surmounting her own sorrows, Susan gathers strength from her daughter, her career and her sole memento of their joy, the locket. The author reveals deep insight into human nature, extensive knowledge of Wales and its traditions, and understanding of the vital role music plays in elevating hearts and minds. Guiding her characters through the depths of despair and the omnipresent shadow of evil, she deftly prepares the reader for a rhapsodic ending.

Emily Cary
Author of *The Loudoun Legacy* and *The Ghost of Whitaker Mountain*

Music breaks through fear and adversity in Janet Litherland's fourth novel, *Song of the Heart*. It is a story of resilience, where the most valuable gift we can possess is the belief and perseverance to insist that creative application of our love and talent always matters. In the end, it is this humble gift that produces a well composed musical score, a beautiful life, and in this case, a great novel. This is Janet's gift in *Song of the Heart*. Don't wait to open it!

Cynthia VanLandingham
Owner, Tally Piano & Keyboard Studios
Tallahassee, Florida

VANISHED

For those of us who were children during the Depression and World War II, *Vanished* brings back many memories. Janet Litherland takes us there with a skill that makes it seem easy. She never uses a long word when a short one will do, nor a paragraph when a simple sentence is enough. She knows Georgia and how her people think and speak, and the dialogue of her characters rings as true as the old courthouse clock. ... *Vanished* skillfully blends this gentleness with the harsh reality of the OSS, the assassination of Italy's brutal dictator Mussolini, and a mysterious disappearance, into an old-fashioned page-turner.

Tex Atkinson
Commander, US Navy (ret.)
Author of *From the Cockpit: Coming of Age in the Korean War*

Intriguing but credible characters and attention to period detail, these are what make a good historical novel. Janet Litherland knows how to craft both. Settle into your favorite chair and drift off to rural Georgia. But be ready for a few surprises.

Ken Libbey
Author of *Vantage Points* and *Midnight in Prague*

CHAIN OF DECEPTION

A completely apt title for this book. As the story progresses, the main character finds out bits and pieces of deception that lead to more questions and even more deception. Keeps the reader turning the pages!

Tami Brady
TCM Reviews

Litherland's authentic characters and careful research succeed brilliantly. ...This insightful journey into the Irish psyche is wise and wondrous and witty.

Arthur L. Zapel
Executive Editor, Meriwether Publishing, Ltd.

DISCOVERY IN TIME

Reads well and pulls you to each new page and chapter like a magnet. One of the best I've read this year.

Dennis
A Reader, PublishAmerica.com

Full of southern charm, local history, past traditions and an interesting web of people. A pure delight from beginning to end!

Customer Review
Amazon.com

SONG OF THE HEART

Janet Litherland

PublishAmerica
Baltimore

ISBN: 1-60703-029-2
PUBLISHED BY PUBLISHAMERICA, LLLP
www.publishamerica.com
Baltimore

Printed in the United States of America

Prelude

The crumpled newspaper lay on the floor, and Susan gave it another sharp kick. Inside it, the dreaded notice screamed silently, as if it were front-page headlines being denied prominence. She'd known it was coming. Several days ago she'd received notification that the most evil man she had ever known would soon be released from prison. All of his victims had been notified. But Susan had been in denial for years; and, once again, she'd stubbornly pushed the subject—*him*—out of her mind. Now it was out there, in print, for the whole world to see! Everything would be dredged up again. Even after all this time, people would remember. Would they talk among themselves? Would they look at her differently?

Just moments ago she'd been anticipating a relaxing evening—good coffee, good music, and the weekend edition of the paper. Now her coffee, steaming from its mug, sat untouched on the table beside her favorite chair, and the London Symphony's version of "Rhapsody on a Theme of Paganini," one of her favorite classical pieces, floated unheard from newly installed surround-sound speakers. Yesterday, Susan Evans had finished recording her own acoustic guitar arrangement of the rhapsody, the final selection for a new CD—her second. Her students at the university had been enthusiastic with encouragement, and her mother's comment that she was "almost famous" had made her smile. She wasn't smiling now.

She hugged herself tightly, aware of her pounding heart, agonizing over what she had just read. That monster's "freedom" had always been in the future, a safe distance from reality. Susan had moved forward over the years, had gone on with life. Her life counted for something! She took a deep breath and let it out slowly. Would he ruin it all now? ...*Could* he? She knew he would try. He'd threatened her—*promised* her—that one day he'd get even.

"It's been nineteen years!" she said aloud, though no one was in the room to hear. She gave the paper another angry kick, her words becoming a whisper: "How could nineteen years pass so quickly?" No longer in denial, she was frightened. Even more frightened than she'd been so long ago. Now there was more at risk…much more to lose.

~ ~ ~

Forrest Fletcher had learned a valuable lesson in prison—keep your mind and ears open and your mouth shut. The latter was difficult for him. As a politician, even a small-town politician, he'd always been ready with a polished line for reporters and constituents, a dazzling smile for the cameras, kisses for babies, and handshakes for everyone, even homeless guys. Yeah, that played well in the press. Some called it "glad-handing," but that didn't bother Fletch. Hey, it was part of the game. But that game wasn't played in prison. He'd tried it once when he first got there, smiling brightly and offering his hand to Big Jim out in the yard. Huh, he'd got his wrist broke. Fletch wasn't stupid. From then on, he'd kept his mouth shut and his hands to himself. His mind, though, he'd kept that wide open. He'd taken advantage of computer classes, studied in the prison library, picked the brains of white-collar inmates, and kept a watchful eye on the guys who were street-smart. Just thinking about that now—everything he'd learned—made his muscles hard. All of them. And his new-found knowledge was just what he needed to finish the job he'd started nineteen years ago. Helloooo, Susan Evans!

Part I
Andante

Chapter 1
Tallahassee, Florida

After a restless night, doing more thinking than sleeping, Susan Evans was up early. As she stood in her comfortable living room, watching gentle rain land in soft "plops" against the window, she absently fingered the locket that hung from her neck. She often touched it or pressed it to her heart or her face, sometimes even kissed it, but in times of stress she never failed to reach for it. The newspaper, closed against the offender-notification, lay at her feet. She had not gone near it since the night before. If there were anything at all to be thankful for, it was the law prohibiting that pervert from contacting his victims. Not that he wouldn't try. She'd never forget the way he'd snarled and threatened her, as he was led away in handcuffs. He'd been a big-shot city councilman and Susan had been responsible for his arrest. Since he couldn't, or wouldn't, accept his own guilt, he'd blamed her for ruining his life. ...But she had not let him ruin hers.

The sun began poking its head through gray-blue clouds, turning the raindrops into brief kaleidoscopes of color. *Rain, sun. Rain, sun. Just like life,* Susan thought. She was definitely in "rain mode" now, though just yesterday she'd been sunshine itself, zipping through life at top speed. Then last night she'd been frightened, even terrified. Her fright had quickly turned to anger, then denial, then anger again. Now she was just plain worried, not to mention exhausted after very little sleep. As she watched the sun and rain play their games, her fingers caressed the locket...back and forth, back and forth.

"What is it, Mom?" her daughter, Anwen, asked from the doorway. "Did my coffee ruin your appetite?" The question was rhetorical, only meant to open a conversation; hopefully, one with some depth. Anwen pulled a footstool up close to Susan's chair and sat on it. "Come, sit with me," she said, motioning to the empty chair.

Susan managed a bright smile and turned toward her only child, who was now an eighteen-year-old grownup. "Oh, Annie darling, you make great coffee. You know that!" Susan, whose profession required a practiced charm, could switch from gloom to glitter in an instant. But Anwen wasn't fooled.

"Mom, whenever I see you with that far-off, sad look in your eyes, you have hold of your locket. Could we…could we finally, after all these years, talk about it?"

Susan gasped and looked down at her hand as if unaware of what it held. She let go of the locket and sat, gripping the arms of her chair. "It's not that, Annie. It's just…well, after working so hard and long to record that CD, it's finally finished and I don't have a lot to do." *Liar*, she told herself. *You are lying to your daughter.*

Anwen knew that Susan's moods had nothing to do with music. She thought her mother was the most beautiful, vivacious woman in the world and seemed even younger than her thirty-seven years. She also could play classical guitar a lot better—in Annie's opinion—than any of the more prominent musicians of the day. Anwen wanted her mother to be happy all of the time, not just sometimes. Susan moved in a busy world, full of interesting people, yet during the quiet times she seemed…well, lonely.

"Hey, Mom, this is *me* you're trying to con. You have guitar students at the university, plus a concert coming up in two weeks with one horrendous rehearsal schedule ahead—you have plenty to do! It's the locket, or whatever it represents, that has you down. Again. …You've never shown me what's inside."

Susan looked out the window, not responding. The locket had nothing to do with her mood, her fear. The locket was her source of comfort. Touching it in times of trouble was instinctive, automatic. It represented something good, something she would never forget, something she wished with all her heart she could reclaim.

"Look at me, Mom."

Susan turned to her. "Annie…"

"I'm an adult now. I can handle it, whatever it is." More gently, she added, "Maybe I can even help. Tell me, Mom. Please."

Susan had to smile. "I remember the last time you asked me about the locket," she said. "You were just ten years old. You wanted to know if it held a picture of the man who fathered you."

"And you said No. Just that—No."

14

Susan's smile broadened to a grin. "And then, my brassy young daughter asked me if she was the result of an affair!"

Anwen rolled her eyes. "I barely knew what the word meant. But I'm glad you set me straight."

Susan remembered that long-ago conversation as if it were yesterday. She had said:

"It wasn't an affair, Annie."

"Well, what was it then? You never talk about my father. Nothing good; nothing bad. Is he alive? What's his name? What's my name? Everyone calls you Mrs. Evans, but that can't be true because Granny's name is Evans. Your name is the same as your mother's!"

"And yours is the same as mine. You are Anwen Elizabeth Evans. I love you very much, darling. I've never told you lies, and I won't start now."

"No, you just won't tell me anything, and that's the same as lying. . . . Were you even married when I was born?"

"Annie, come sit beside me, let me put my arm around you. . . . It's time you knew, and I hope it doesn't upset you too much."

"No lies?"

"No lies. . . . Here, give me your hand. . . . The man who fathered you—I will never refer to him as your father—is in prison. He was sent there for raping me when I was a teenager. Do you know what rape is?"

"Umhmm, sort of. I know what makes babies. You told me about not letting anyone touch me in my private places. And our teacher at school told us in health class if anyone tried, we should say No and mean it."

"Well, I said No and I meant it; but he was older, and he had given me some. . . well, some sleeping medicine without my knowledge. I fought him and cried until I was too tired to cry or fight any more. Then I went to sleep. When I woke up, I was scared and confused, and I was very upset. The man owned a business in the town where we lived then, back in Georgia, and everyone liked him.

"In Davenport, where Grandpa and Granny live?"

"Yes. Before the man let me out of the car, he warned me not to tell anyone. He said that no one would believe my word over his, that my reputation would be ruined. . . . But I chose to tell. And when I did, other young girls said he had hurt them too, and that man was sent to prison for a very long time. So you see, Annie, he's not your father and he never will be; but what happened that night gave me you—the most precious thing in my life. . . . Here, now, no tears, sweetheart."

"Do I look like him?"

"Not one bit. He's a redhead, and you're a blonde, like me. You know how everyone says you look just like me."

"I'm glad. I don't want to look like him. But...but, will I grow up to be bad like him?"

"Absolutely not! You're a wonderful girl, and I love you and will always take care of you. You also have Grandpa and Gran, and Aunt Beth and Uncle Joel who love you like their own. There's no way you can be anything other than the sweet girl you are."

"You never mentioned our conversation again," Annie said.

Susan shook her head. "No. For a long time after the attack, I kept thinking about what I could have done differently. Maybe just one little thing would have changed the outcome. I did say No. I thought it was supposed to stop when I said No. But I'd been drugged and couldn't put up much of a fight. I tried to forget about it. Later, after you and I talked, I just didn't believe that hashing and rehashing it would do any good or change anything for me, or for us. No, Annie, I didn't mention it again. Finally, I put the whole thing where it belonged—in the past. It was over and done with."

"I remember feeling disappointed that my father—sorry, the 'man who fathered me'—was a bad man. Actually, I went to my room to think about it. But then Marlena came and wanted me to go with her for some ice cream." Annie smiled wryly. "As a child, the ice cream was more important."

"I knew you were upset, because you had forgotten about the question that started it all, asking me what was in the locket. In fact, you haven't asked about my locket since we had that conversation—eight, almost nine, years ago."

"I was afraid to. Afraid it might stir up more bad memories. Mom, look— you have hold of it again. Tell me about that pretty piece of jewelry. Tell me the truth this time. ...Please."

Slowly, Susan unfastened the clasp, removed the gold chain from her neck, opened the tiny compartment, and handed the locket to her daughter. Maybe it would distract Anwen from her mother's fear. Maybe it would distract them both.

"This locket represents one of the happiest times in my life, two years before the...the *incident* with the man who fathered you. I was sixteen years old and in love for the first...no, for the *only* time in my life," Susan said. "His name was Rhys Llewellyn and he lived in Wales." Her eyes began to mist. "I met him when my high school literary group went there on an educational trip."

"Wales! You did tell me about that trip and how much fun it was. That was why you chose a Welsh name for me—Anwen—in memory of your visit to Wales."

"All true."

"But you never said anything about meeting someone special while you were there."

"Too painful."

"And now?"

"Sad. ...I feel sad."

Anwen looked down at the two photographs inside the locket. On the left was a young version of her mother—smooth skin, bright eyes, long blond hair, and a brilliant smile. And on the right was a darkly handsome boy with equally bright eyes, looking adoringly across the tiny hinge toward Susan. It was obvious from the background that the two photos had originally been one, cut apart to fit into the apertures. The subjects may have been very young, but there was no mistaking the love and laughter illuminating their eyes. It was genuine, and Anwen was captivated.

"Have you been in touch with this boy? I mean, this man? What did you say his name was?"

"It's pronounced Reese, spelled R-h-y-s. I don't know where he is...or even if he's still alive."

Anwen felt a sudden tenderness for her mother, an appreciation for her vulnerability and for what this conversation was costing her. "Well, it's obvious to me that you still care for him," she said gently.

"It's more than that, Annie. I know this sounds silly after twenty-one years, but I still *love* him." Finally, the tears spilled onto Susan's cheeks. "...I've never loved anyone else."

~   ~   ~

The locket had successfully distracted Anwen, at least for the present, and talking about it gave her mother some measure of comfort. But it could not erase Susan's underlying emotion: Fear. The "respected businessman" who had raped her nearly nineteen years ago would soon be out of prison, free to roam the streets, free to...Forrest Fletcher was, indeed, someone to be feared.

Chapter 2
Trefriw, Wales: July 1987

"I think he likes you, Susan," the young violinist whispered as the girls placed their instruments in the room that would be locked for safe-keeping.

"Don't be silly," Susan whispered back with a shy smile. Nevertheless, she glanced over her shoulder to see if he looked her way. He did. She quickly turned attention to her acoustic guitar, putting it lovingly into its case. It had been a gift from her Uncle Fred on her eleventh birthday, along with lessons from a good teacher, and had been her passion for the past five years.

"He's really cute," Angie continued, not letting the subject go. "And he directs his comments to you most of the time, as if the rest of us aren't even here. Lucky you!" She giggled and covered her mouth.

The *he* she referred to was their tour guide, whose badge read, "Rhys Llewellyn, Snowdonia Tours, Conwy." He had joined the group of eight students and their chaperones at a pretty church in Trefriw, a quaint little village cut into the side of a mountain in the northern part of the country.

Four musicians and four artists of exceptional talent and academic standing, soon to be juniors at Brookfield, a private high school in Davenport, Georgia, had earned an educational/artistic excursion to the Festival of Music & the Arts in Llandudno on the north coast of Wales, an annual event in that country since 1945. This year the Festival would incorporate a "Celebration of Youth."

They had arrived in Trefriw the day before, because one of the students, Catrin Fenna, had moved to the United States from Wales six years earlier, and her grandparents still lived in the village. It seemed a good place, a logical place, for the group to begin their adventure.

"Many lessons packed into a few days," Mr. Fleetwood, their music teacher, had said, promising a test when they returned home. "Not only a test on what you observe at the festival, but also on all things Welsh. So keep your eyes and ears open," he'd warned. He and his wife, who was their art teacher, served as chaperones, and the students adored both of them.

That evening the musicians—two violinists, a flutist and a classical guitarist—would play a short recital in the gathering room at the church Catrin Fenna had attended with her family as a child in Trefriw, and the four young artists would display their work. Morning preparations had gone well, and Rhys Llewellyn had arrived to conduct a tour of the area. He would be with them for the entire ten days, guiding them through the Festival and introducing them to the history and artistry of Wales.

"Move, Susan!" Angie chided. "You can't stay in this tiny room with your back to *him* all day."

Susan moved, knowing that her friend was right—Rhys did pay special attention to her. And she loved it! He was just about the best-looking boy she'd ever seen. With his nearly black hair and snapping dark eyes, he reminded her of Pierce Brosnan, who played "Remington Steele" on TV. Susan's older sister, Beth, always made *ooo-ing* noises when Brosnan came on the screen. Unfortunately, the show's run had ended the previous year; but Beth still made noises whenever his name came up.

"How old do you suppose he is?" Angie asked.

"Who?"

"Rhys!"

"I don't know. Maybe nineteen."

"If he's twenty, he's too old; but he's still cute."

"We're having lunch at the café at Bodnant Garden, just north of here," Rhys announced as the group gathered on the wide stone steps outside the church. "Then we'll visit the garden and return to Trefriw for a bit o' rest before your concert."

"Don't you love to hear him talk?" Angie whispered to Susan, elbowing her. "His accent is adorable!"

"Shh!" Susan was embarrassed; but, yes, she did love to hear him talk. And she didn't really think that twenty was too old.

Their guide continued, "I understand you won't be having an evening meal until after your concert, so I suggest you eat a hearty lunch. Everyone into the van now! Our driver, Mr. Narberth, is waiting."

19

The students and their chaperones climbed into a shiny white, fifteen-passenger van with "Snowdonia Tours" painted on each side in green letters. Susan's heart fluttered as Rhys helped her in, his hand on her arm. Cautiously, she looked into those wicked eyes of his…and he winked! *Oh, my gosh!* she thought, sure that her face had turned three shades of red.

He read her nametag aloud, "Susan Evans." And smiled.

She returned the smile, then quickly found a seat near the back and settled nervously into it. Scott, the boy who sat next to the window, said to her, "Maybe I should paint a picture of that for my art display."

Susan looked out the window. "Of what?"

Scott and Susan had been friends since grade school, and now he was grinning. "Of the way that tour guide looks at you. You s'pose that's typical Welsh?"

She poked him playfully, still embarrassed.

~   ~   ~

Rhys Llewellyn took his seat in the front of the van, picked up his microphone, and began describing the countryside, occasionally injecting bits of Welsh humor. Good thing he had it memorized, though, because his mind wasn't on the spiel. He was thinking of the beautiful brown-eyed girl in the back of the van and how his heart had nearly stopped when she looked straight into his eyes. *Blond hair and brown eyes*, he thought. *A smashing combination!* He'd first noticed her during morning rehearsal, as she played the sweetest sounds he'd ever heard coming from a guitar. "The Gentle Bird," it was, a beautiful Welsh tune he'd only before heard played on a harp. Rhys watched the way she'd bent over her instrument, lifted her head, shook it a bit, totally absorbed in her music. He was drawn to her devotion and wondered what it would be like to receive such devotion from another human being. From *her*. …In his short life, he hadn't experienced devotion of any kind.

"Notice the sheep-dotted fields," he said in his practiced tour-guide voice. "Very important to the woolen mills hereabouts. You'll be visiting Trefriw's mill tomorrow morning." Earlier, Susan had dipped her feet in the clear stream that ran down the mountain alongside the woolen mill.

"Oh, and have you noticed the unpronounceable place names since you've been in Wales? Dyffryn? Ynysybwl? Tywyn?" Rhys was treated to a chorus of groans. "Or my own surname, Llewellyn. My ancestors had to throw in a couple of 'E's' just so you Americans could pronounce it."

Scott chuckled and looked at Susan, who was enthralled by the commentary.

Rhys continued: "The Welsh are not too fond of vowels, 'tis true. Someone once said that a few hundred years ago, a boatload of Welshmen moved to your own state of Hawaii and took all the vowels with them." The teachers laughed immediately, followed closely by the students as they caught on.

Soon, they pulled into the shady and hilly car park at Bodnant Garden. Rhys helped each student exit the van, giving Susan's arm a special squeeze. He liked the way she looked at him—such a beautiful smile.

"Go directly to the tea room," he instructed the group, indicating a small wooden structure with an inviting porch. "Tables have been set for you inside."

When the students entered, they found a surprise waiting, though it was no surprise to Rhys. He'd planned it. A Welsh harpist was entertaining at one end of the room. He was playing "All I Ask of You" from *Phantom of the Opera*. The students stopped just inside the door, captivated by the beautiful music exquisitely performed.

"Go ahead to the counter and collect your lunches," Rhys instructed, "then bring them to the tables. The harpist will keep playing as long as you're here. You won't miss a beat."

Susan held back from the group and spoke to Rhys. "This is wonderful," she whispered to him, not wanting to disturb the musician. "Did you know he'd be here?"

Rhys's eyes sparkled, turning Susan's insides to butter. "Of course. He is a very promising young artist with a great career ahead of him. I'm glad you like the surprise."

"Like it? I *love* it! He's magnificent!"

Just then the harpist switched to another tune, slower and more reverent-sounding. "What is he playing now?" Susan asked.

Rhys laughed. "Oddly enough, it's called 'Rhys,' though it has nothing at all to do with me. 'Tis a Welsh hymn."

The two of them collected their lunches from the counter and found seats at the tables. Together, of course.

~ ~ ~

After lunch, the students wandered about the garden on their own, breaking into small units. Angie, Scott, and Susan explored together, enjoying both the formal lawns on the upper level and the wild spaces below. Rhys joined them for a walk through the Laburnum Arch, a long tunnel of golden blooms. Scott and Angie moved slightly ahead, giving Rhys and Susan a little time alone.

21

"This is so beautiful!" Susan exclaimed, looking at the shimmering flowers.

"Yes, it is," Rhys replied, looking only at Susan.

"Have you been doing this for a long time? Leading tours, I mean."

"Well, not too long," he replied, "since I'm only eighteen."

Susan rewarded him with her brilliant smile, delighted that he was only two years older than herself. "You know what I mean," she teased.

"This is my third summer as a guide," he said. "And, now that I've graduated school, I'm working for Snowdonia Tours full time."

"I heard Mr. Narberth, our driver, call you the 'golden boy.' Why is that?"

Rhys laughed. "Ah, everyone around the company does. It's because of what they call my 'high and mighty ideas,' though they mean it kindly and cheer me on. Even the owner of Snowdonia Tours encourages me to be his competitor."

"Competitor?"

He nodded. "Someday I hope to own a tour company with several vans and guides. That's a wide-open field of work in the British Isles. Always tourists wanting to see things. . . . What about you? What are your plans?"

Susan sighed. "No plans yet, just dreams. I won't graduate until the spring of eighty-nine. After that, I'd really like to study classical guitar at the university; however, as my mother has often pointed out, that won't be a particularly useful degree if I intend to support myself."

"University? That would be very nice." He looked away. "Unfortunately, it's not an option for me."

She put her hand on his arm. "But to own your own business—that's exciting!"

"You think so?" He turned back to her. "I've got it all worked out—how much capital I'll need, how to acquire financing; even wrote my business plan."

"I admire you," she said, simply. And she meant it. "To have the nerve to go into business for yourself. Wow!" Her hand was still on his arm, but she quickly removed it.

"Susan, do you. . .would you. . .would it be possible for us to have dinner together this evening after your recital?" he asked. "I mean. . .I know you have to stay with someone from your group, but maybe they—" He pointed ahead to Angie and Scott. "Maybe the four of us could be together."

Susan's heart started to pound. He wanted to be with her—Susan Evans. This handsome, fascinating boy wanted to be with *her*! "Y-yes," she replied. "Yes, I'm sure we could work it out."

Chapter 3

The recital was short but very nice, and fifty-two people attended. "The whole population of Trefriw," Rhys had joked. Afterward, three local families provided a picnic, with bottles of lemonade; and the students along with a few Trefriw teenagers, new friends, split into small units of two or three, carrying their food to various places in the little mountain village—benches, low walls, grassy terraces.

Susan knew she shouldn't have slipped away with Rhys, but Angie had encouraged her. "I'll cover for you," Angie said, giving her friend a push. So Susan and Rhys began walking, passing quaint shops built of rock, some whitewashed like the Gwesty Fairy Falls Hotel, all sitting very close to the road. As they started to cross, Rhys caught her arm and reminded her to "look right" for traffic, not left, since cars would be approaching from what Susan had called the "wrong side of the road."

"It's not the wrong side in Wales," he said, laughing. "Our drivers also sit on the right side of the auto, you know."

"You mean the wrong side."

"I mean the *correct* side." He squeezed her hand, pulling her closer to him as they walked beneath the trees. Darkness had fallen, but the light from each other's eyes was all that was needed. Susan had never felt so...so much the object of anyone's attention. He looked at her. He talked directly to her. He cared about her. She could tell. And it frightened and excited her at the same time. When finally they stepped behind a tree and he kissed her, she thought she would have a melt-down. Rhys's kiss sent streaks of fire from her head straight down through the core of her body until even her toes were tingling!

"Susan, this...this is new to me. I just want you to know," Rhys said, his lips close to her ear. "I've never...what do you Americans say—'come on'—to anyone like this before. I'm kind of embarrassed. Actually, I'm a quiet sort, really I am."

"So am I, Rhys. I'm so dumb about stuff like this; I don't even know what to say or do. But I do know that I like you very much, and I feel wonderful just being with you."

His mouth suddenly broke into a wide smile and he asked, "Do you think…could you, or rather would you…play your guitar for me?"

Susan took a step back. "…Now?"

"Now. Just for me."

"Well, sure, I guess so. If the church is still open. Oh, but the instruments are locked up."

"Pedr's still there, the custodian. He knows me. It's a way for us to be together longer," he explained.

She smiled and nodded; and Rhys cupped her face in his hands, pulled her closer, and kissed her once again. "You're wonderful," he said.

They emerged from the trees holding hands but quickly stepped apart lest anyone should see them. Across the street they climbed the hill to the church and let themselves in. Susan was excited. She had never in her life felt like this. She wanted to spend a long time with Rhys, and a private "concert"—she giggled at the thought—was a great idea!

The custodian was in the gathering room, sweeping, and he looked up as they entered. "Well, hello there, young Rhys," he said, leaning on his broomstick. "And what brings you back here after hours? Shouldn't you be doing your touristy business?"

Rhys laughed. "That's what I'm doing, Pedr. Touristy business. This young lady wants to practice her guitar some more. Would you open the storeroom for her, please?"

"Well, since you asked so nice, I guess I could." He put his broom aside, hiked up his pants, and sauntered toward the storeroom door. "How long you plan to be here, Miss?" he asked Susan.

"Uh, not long."

"She's just going to play a few tunes," Rhys said. "Wants to correct some mistakes she made in the concert tonight."

"Umhmm." The man turned to the door and unlocked it.

Susan elbowed Rhys in the ribs, mouthing the word *mistakes*?

He grinned and winked at her. "Thanks, Pedr," he said.

Susan retrieved her guitar. "Yes, thank you," she added.

"You can't stay long, mind you. I'll only be here for about twenty more minutes, then I'm locking up."

"That's fine, Pedr," Rhys said, guiding Susan toward the archway on his right. "We'll just go into this little anteroom and leave you to your work."

"Umhmm. Touristy business is it? More like monkey business, if you ask me." He pointed his finger at Rhys. "Good thing I know you, young Rhys. You're a good boy. Stay that way!" Pedr returned to his broom, then called over his shoulder, "I'll have me ear on you!"

The young couple settled into the comfortable little room, leaving the door open for Pedr's "ear." Susan took her guitar from its case. "Anything in particular you'd like to hear?" she asked.

"Yes. 'The Gentle Bird.' When I heard you play it earlier, I couldn't believe my ears. It's a Welsh harp tune, and you're an American guitarist!"

Susan's face lit up. "I learned it especially for this trip. Mr. Fleetwood said it would be nice to play something from this country. He wrote the guitar arrangement himself."

"A wise man. You're going to be a big hit at the festival in Llandudno, Susan."

As she tuned the strings, she asked, innocently, "Is this the song I made mistakes in?"

Rhys laughed aloud. "I guess you won't be letting me forget that."

"Not likely." She smiled and began to play. After two more songs, she started "The Rose," singing the words as she played. Rhys thought it the most beautiful music he'd ever heard. She played like an angel; she sang like an angel. *She is an angel*, he thought.

She finished singing, "...the seed that with the sun's love in the spring becomes the rose," and plucked the final notes. For a few seconds the room was very quiet, the two young people gazing at each other; then Pedr, the custodian, coughed discreetly from the doorway.

"Time to lock up," he said, and turned away.

Susan put her guitar back in its case and, as she stood, Rhys gently kissed her forehead. "Thank you," he whispered. "It was beautiful. You are beautiful."

As they exited the church, they could see Angie waiting at the foot of the hill. Quickly, Rhys pulled Susan into the darkness of the trees alongside the path and whispered into her ear, "I meant what I said. You are a beautiful angel." His lips moved from her ear around to her face, planting tiny kisses as he sought her mouth. She threw her arms around him, and this time their kiss was not tentative. It was full and strong, and when they emerged from the trees just a few kisses later…they were in love.

~ ~ ~

Fifty events were packed into the week-long Llandudno Festival, many overlapping; so Mr. and Mrs. Fleetwood had selected the music and art activities they felt would benefit their group most, including a "talk" by Welsh artist Peter Prendergast; a concert sponsored by the Ratcliff Foundation (organ, strings and voices); the "Vision of Wales" art exhibition; a lunchtime concert by the Gwynedd Youth Jazz Orchestra, and the Senior Instrumental Competition, though they would not be competing. Additionally, Rhys was challenged to show them places of interest.

"We'll be visiting the Oriel Mostyn Gallery this afternoon, showing contemporary art by major artists, not only from Wales but around the world," Rhys explained to the group gathered in front of the Clarence Hotel in Llandudno where they were staying. "They've a craft shop there where you can purchase souvenirs. Also, on the last day—something special—we'll be walking the Great Orme."

"That's a mountain!" Scott cried, evoking laughter from the others.

"Nah, just a huge rock. An easy ramble. You'll find evidence of ancient settlements, and stone circles reminiscent of Stonehenge. Lot's o' history there."

"Yeah, Scott, you'll have to pass a test on it," Catrin chided.

"Easy for you to say. You probably walked it in diapers!"

"You mean nappies?" Rhys asked, and everyone giggled. "We've also planned some swimming and a bit o' ten-pin bowling this week," he said. "No test on those."

Rhys flashed a smile at Susan, and she thought she might collapse. All she could think of was his kiss the night before. His *many* kisses. And tender touches. …She shivered.

~ ~ ~

Susan thought the daily music and art sessions were fabulous, and the extra activities Rhys planned for them were fun. Each night, contrary to her rather strict upbringing, she snuck out of the hotel to meet Rhys. Angie helped her and was ready to cover for her if Mrs. Fleetwood came looking, which (thankfully!) she never did. Their meetings were innocent, never more than kissing, hugging, and a little experimental touching, which frightened Susan at first—in a goodway, that is. And each evening their parting was more difficult, lingering, tender…

Finally, the last night arrived. They stood in the shadows across the street from the Clarence Hotel. Except for the street lamps shrouded in mist, and a few window lights twinkling in the distance, the night was very dark.

"Tomorrow, after our trip to the Great Orme," Rhys said, "I have to take your group to the train station. This is our last time to be together."

"I know." She was trembling, trying not to cry.

"Do you know I love you?"

She nodded and the tears fell.

"It's okay," he said, kissing her tears away. "We'll write to each other. We'll talk about our dreams, make plans. It won't be long, sweetheart. We'll be together again."

"I have two more years of high school!" she cried.

"And I have a business to build. Be strong, Susan. Maybe I can visit you in the States. Maybe next year even."

"R-really?"

"It's possible." He swallowed hard, knowing he didn't have an extra pence in his pocket. Didn't matter. They could dream. He loved this girl. Always would.

Their last kiss was soft, sweet…a kiss to remember.

~   ~   ~

Late the next afternoon at the top of Great Orme, Scott acknowledged that the climb "wasn't so bad"—in fact, they'd ridden a cable car most of the way. Ever the artist, he began taking pictures, awed by the view. Suddenly Angie tapped him on the shoulder and pointed. Susan and Rhys stood side by side, looking out over the blue waters of Conwy Bay.

"Get their picture," Angie urged. "Hey, you two! Turn around!"

They turned and Scott clicked. Surprised, they looked at each other and laughed. And he clicked again. It was a great shot; nevertheless, Scott rolled his eyes at the "young lovers" concept. Couldn't help it.

"I want a copy of that," Rhys said.

"So do I," Susan echoed.

"You think I took it for myself?" Scott winked at Susan. Later, he whispered so only she could hear, "Some trip, huh?"

Oddly enough, she wasn't embarrassed. "Yeah…some trip."

Chapter 4
Tallahassee, Florida

"So that's where these photos were taken," Anwen said, holding the locket, gazing at the pictures of her mother and Rhys Llewellyn. "On top of a mountain!"

"The Great Orme."

"Amazing!"

"Actually, it's one photo," Susan said. "I cut it apart to fit into the sides of the locket. Your grandfather gave me the locket for my sixteenth birthday; but I never showed him, or Mom, what I put in it. …A little too revealing, don't you think?"

Anwen laughed. "I'd say that love is pretty obvious. Did you ever tell them about meeting Rhys?"

"Not really. I said I'd met some new friends in Wales, to explain why I was writing letters frequently. Of course they knew Catrin Fenna and her parents and thought that connecting with her grandparents in Trefriw was special for all of us."

"That's a wonderful story, Mom. But what happened? Why didn't the two of you get together later on?"

"…Rhys stopped writing. Exactly one year later, he stopped writing. He sent me a short note—I'll never forget it—it said, 'This is my last letter, Susan. Something unfortunate has happened here, and I am leaving Snowdonia. You are beautiful and talented, and you deserve much more than I could ever give you. Please remember that I love you. We are soul mates, and I will love you forever.' Forever was underlined."

Susan's eyes filled with tears. "I still have the note…and all of his other letters.

They're buried in the bottom of my jewelry chest along with the gift he sent me that first Christmas. Would you...would you like to see the gift?"

Anwen knew that her mother needed to talk, to share. "Of course. I would love to see it."

They went to Susan's bedroom, where Susan took a fold of tissue paper from her jewelry chest. She opened it and lifted out a small wooden spoon, holding it in the palm of her hand. "It's a lovespoon," she said. "It's the custom in Wales for a young man to give one to his sweetheart as a token of affection." The handle was intricately carved with daffodils entwined in Celtic knots. "Actually, in the old days a young man would do the carving himself, but they don't any more; there are such pretty ones to buy."

"It's beautiful," Anwen said. "What a special gift!" It was so delicate that she was reluctant to touch it.

"He loved me, Annie. I know he did. I do know that something awful happened to him. Otherwise, he wouldn't have stopped writing. At this point, I don't even know if he's still alive."

"Did you try to reach him back then?"

"Of course I did. I wrote several more times, but my letters were returned by the post office." She removed a packet from the bottom of the chest. "His letters are here, every one he ever wrote me," she said, fingering the mauve ribbon that held them together. "I also tried calling, but his phone was disconnected."

"Did you contact the tour company he worked for? What was it called? Conway something?"

"Conwy. Snowdonia Tours, Conwy. Yes, I wrote them. I couldn't very well make international calls. I was only sixteen, and my parents would not have understood." Susan absently tucked a stray lock of hair behind her ear. "They were nice about letting me call Rhys that first Christmas, though. But I didn't tell them that Rhys was a boy—just a friend in Wales."

"Did you hear from them? The people at the tour company?" Annie prodded.

"Yes, a secretary sent me a nice letter saying Rhys had left the company and moved away. She had no idea where. I even asked Catrin to contact her grandparents to see if they had heard anything."

"And...?"

"At first, all she could tell me was that he was gone and didn't want to be found. I guess she, or her grandparents, didn't want me to feel worse than I already did. When I kept pressuring her, she finally said that he had been accused of something, but everyone was sure he hadn't done it. Catrin had no idea what it was about. All her grandmother would say was, 'A crying shame, what happened to young Rhys.' By the time it was over, Rhys apparently was despondent and felt that his friends had let him down. Either they had not been convinced of his innocence or didn't want to get involved. So he left the area." Susan turned to her daughter. "He was so *alone*, Annie!"

"That's awful. What about his parents, his family?"

"He was an orphan. He lived at Arnhall, an orphanage in Llandudno, until it closed in 1981. He was twelve then, and was sent to a couple of foster homes. I don't know where. ...But, Annie, he was so smart, so determined. The tour-guide job he'd had for three summers, and then full time, enabled him to move out on his own as soon as he turned eighteen. He was very proud of what he'd been able to accomplish by himself. He wanted to build a tour business and had it all down on paper, exactly how he intended to do it. ...My heart aches for him. It's been aching for twenty-one years."

"Did you try an Internet search?"

"Annie," Susan said wryly, "that was 1988. The Internet was not easily available in private homes then, as it is now."

"I mean, have you tried a search recently?"

"I tried several months ago, but you know I'm not Internet savvy. And I..." She looked down at her hands. "I didn't want to ask anyone for help. There are probably zillions of Rhys Llewellyns all over the world anyway. I have no idea where to begin."

"Well I *am* Internet savvy! Why don't we start a search now?"

"N-now?"

Anwen took her mother by the arm. "Come on. Let's go to my room and log on. Isn't twenty-one years long enough to wait?"

~   ~   ~

"This is crazy," Susan said, as she pulled up a chair beside Anwen and peered over her shoulder, yet her eyes were bright with excitement. "He's probably happily married and has a bunch of kids. I shouldn't intrude in his life."

"Let's look at it this way: You don't plan to intrude. You just want to know. There's no harm in knowing. ...Is there?"

"I guess not. It would relieve my mind, one way or the other."

"Okay. I'm going to do the free stuff first; then if we don't find him, we'll go for a paid search."

"Paid? How much?"

Anwen was intent on her computer screen. "You can afford it," she said absently.

After about thirty minutes of watching futile searches, Susan picked up her packet of letters and wandered out through the back door. She'd recently had a deck built, with benches all around and steps leading to her flower garden. She loved flowers, but her schedule of rehearsals, concerts, and teaching left her no time to tend it. Now, she regretted more than ever that a lawn service had to take care of her yard. Together, she and Annie managed the inside of the house, but that would soon change. Annie was enrolled as a freshman communication major at Florida State University—Susan's alma mater—and would be starting in September. She'd be moving in with a girlfriend…and out of Susan's house.

Susan sighed. *Ah…the empty nest.* The thought made her heart feel like a bowling ball.

"I'll still be in Tallahassee," Annie had said. "We can visit back and forth."

But it won't be the same. Nothing will ever be the same. Then her thoughts turned to Forrest Fletcher's impending release from prison, and the heaviness in her heart became nearly unbearable. Her only consolation was that he was imprisoned in Georgia, a state that was very tough on sex offenders, even after their parole or release from prison. Fletcher would be monitored. *But he has such an ego*, she thought. *What if he thinks of a way to evade the law? What if he tries to find me? What if he suspects Annie is his daughter and approaches her?* Those were not idle thoughts.

"I won't forget this!" he'd growled at her as he was sentenced to nineteen years without parole. "You ruined my life!" he'd shouted.

Susan didn't move or respond, but she thought: *And you tried to ruin mine, and the lives of several other young girls too, you evil creep!*

~ ~ ~

Forrest Fletcher had been a crop-duster pilot in Davenport, Georgia, where Susan and her older sister, Beth, had grown up. By age twenty-eight he owned three planes and had five employees, air and ground. Still unmarried at age thirty, he was a member of the city council and a trustee at a local church. *Such an upstanding citizen*, Susan remembered with bitterness.

Susan had just graduated high school with honors and was giving an evening recital at the home of Theresa Malone, one of her mother's friends. Forty people were in attendance, including locally prominent people, and one of those was Forrest Fletcher.

"Hi, I'm Fletch," he'd said, introducing himself as guests mingled following the concert. He'd just been elected to the council, the youngest ever to achieve membership.

"I know," Susan replied, shyly. "Your picture's always in the paper. Oh, I'm sorry. I shouldn't have said that." She felt stupid, because he was important. And he was cute, though quite a bit older than she.

"That's okay. I really enjoyed your music. How long have you been playing?"

The polite conversation went on for a few minutes, until the hostess guided Susan to others who wanted to speak with her. A little later, Fletch reappeared with an extra cup of punch and held it out to her.

"For you. I'll bet your throat's dry from all this talk."

Susan smiled and gratefully accepted the drink. She thought Fletch was a nice guy. In the past year she'd thought very little about boys, other than Rhys, whom she still loved fervently; and the few dates she'd had...well, they just hadn't measured up. *If only Rhys would write to me*, she thought. Even though it had been two years since her visit to Wales, and one year since she'd last heard from him, she couldn't get him out of her mind and heart. *If only I knew where he was. I want him to know I still love him!* Those were her thoughts as she stood beside Forrest Fletcher at the party.

The following weekend Fletcher called and invited her to a movie. "'Driving Miss Daisy' is playing downtown. It's supposed to be really good. Would you like to go?"

She hesitated, thinking he was too old for her, but then she accepted, rationalizing that she had just turned eighteen and was old enough to make up her own mind. Plus, her best friend—Angie Freeman, who'd been with her in Wales and was now a substitute violinist with the Tallahassee Symphony—had been urging her to get out more. "Your personality is suffering, Susan," Angie had said. "You need to go with some guys now and then. I hate to say it, but you've got to get over Rhys."

Never, she thought. *I'll never get over Rhys! But I will go out with Fletch. He seems nice enough; and safe, being an older man.*

Her father had misgivings. "However," he said, "Fletcher's reputation is impeccable. I suppose you'll be all right."

And she was. They had a good time at the movie, bought some pizza afterward, and he took her home. Didn't even try to kiss her.

But the second date was different. He took her to Albany, a city about eighty miles away, to see and hear Billy Joel at the Civic Center. The show was wonderful, and Susan was impressed with the star. He wasn't all show and glitter and fans—he was a true musician, and she could tell at once that his training had been in classical music and technique. Obviously, Fletch had known this, had known that she would be impressed. That was part of *his* technique.

After the concert, they went to a quiet bar where Fletch ordered a beer and Susan asked for a Coke. As they were ready to leave, Susan excused herself to use the ladies' room while Fletch paid the check. When she returned, he stood, holding both their drinks. He handed the Coke to her, and said, "To a very nice evening." She smiled in complete agreement, and finished her drink. Later, she knew—she *knew*—he had put something in her glass before she'd returned to the table.

He drove home by what he called "the scenic route," which led them quickly to an isolated area near the Flint River.

At once, Susan was wary. She hadn't "parked" with a boy since meeting Rhys, and even then they hadn't done anything more than talk and kiss, a few stolen moments beneath the trees in Trefriw and a few times during the festival in Llandudno. Once, they were standing beside the van and had just broken apart, when Mrs. Fleetwood appeared like a poltergeist and motioned Susan into the hotel with a stern, but kind, warning to stay with her group. So at eighteen, still in love with Rhys whom she hadn't seen in two years, Susan remained a virgin— much to Angie's amazement; yes, girls did discuss such things.

"Fletch," she had said, "I'd rather not stop here. Let's go on home." Oddly, she felt a little sleepy.

"Hey, I really like you, Sue," he said, tilting the steering wheel up, out of the way.

"Susan. It-it's Susan. I don't care for the nickname."

"Okay, Susan." He put his arm around her. "I just want to kiss you. You are so beautiful." He brushed her hair back with his other hand and pulled her face toward his.

One kiss, she thought. *One kiss, then we're out of here.*

But the kiss was hard and cold and deep…and frightening. "Please, Fletch," she said, trying to push him away. "Let's go home."

He paid no attention, pulled her body close to his, buried her face against his neck so she could hardly breathe, and cupped her breast in his hand.

"Stop! Stop right now. I-I don't want to do this." She struck out at him as she spoke the words, but her body was losing control, feeling weaker, and definitely not from arousal. She didn't understand where her strength had gone...until she remembered the Coke she'd left unattended less than thirty minutes before. Tears ran down her cheeks, and she lashed out again. But her attempt was feeble and futile.

Forrest Fletcher wasted no time. The last thing Susan saw before losing consciousness was his lecherous face above hers.

"Wake up," he said. "You're home now."

She opened her eyes, horrified.

"Get yourself together," he said. "Try to look decent in case your folks are waiting up for you."

"...You! You, bas—"

"Don't say it. You don't mean it. You enjoyed it; I know you did. By the way, you were the best I've had in a long time."

Susan struggled to get out of the car, but he grabbed her arm. "One more thing," he said. "Don't tell anyone what you *think* happened tonight. You don't know for sure. Besides, no one will believe you. I'm a member of the city council, a businessman and churchgoer—you said yourself that my name is always in the newspaper. And all of the articles that have ever appeared are complimentary. You'll never convince anyone this was anything other than consensual, so don't try. If you do...*your* reputation will be ruined. Nobody will ever want to hear you play your guitar again. Believe me." He released her, and she nearly fell out of the car. "Comb your hair before going in," he added, as he pulled the passenger door shut.

But Susan did not comb her hair, nor did she wipe off the stickiness she felt beneath her clothing. She went straight to her parents, who had been watching television in the den. Crying, she told them everything. And her father, who was a lawyer, immediately took her to the police station, where she pressed charges against the city's most famous, upstanding young citizen. When the story broke, four other girls—two were underage—came forward with similar stories...and Forrest Fletcher went to prison for a very long time.

~   ~   ~

Now, Susan walked the length of her back deck, willing the horrible memory to go away. Though she also had pleasant memories of dating several men, one for nearly six months, she'd never considered marriage to any of them. Marriage left her no escape in case something went wrong—Fletcher had scared her and scarred her. Too, she had never let go of the hope that someday she and Rhys would be reunited. And if she were married—particularly in a solid, comfortable marriage—that reunion could not happen, because she would not want to hurt the man she had married. She knew that there were different ways to love someone, different kinds of love, but she had never been "in love" the way she'd been in love with Rhys. Yes, she'd only been sixteen years old—"going on seventeen," she'd told herself, recalling the song from *The Sound of Music*—but she was sure of her feelings. And those feelings had not dissipated. If anything, they had intensified over the years, sustaining her belief that she and Rhys had placed an imprint on each other's hearts, that they were true soul mates.

With tears in her eyes, she sat on the bench in the corner of her deck and loosened the tattered ribbon that bound Rhys's letters.

Chapter 5

Susan chose a few letters at random and read parts of them, as if for the first time. In her mind she could hear his voice as it sounded all those years ago, his softly accented words.

> *Dear Susan,*
> *I should have my tour business operating in about a year, two at most, and I hope you'll be able to "cross the pond" at that time! Such a journey won't be an option for me until I've established myself. I know that you have schooling to complete. But we can dream, can't we? I hope you miss me too, just a little.*

Just a little? More like forever. She'd never stopped missing him, loving him. Susan folded that letter and put it away, removing another.

> *Dear Susan,*
> *I have a benefactor! Mr. Siam Whittal has offered to help me get started in business, to match whatever I manage to earn and save on my own. Already, I've nearly a thousand pounds. If I can save another thousand and he matches me, there'll be four thousand pounds to work with. I can lease a van, buy a little promotion and hire a part-time helper. I can build the business quickly—I know I can!*
> *Dream with me, Susan. Make plans to join me, at least to "look me over" once again to see if you still care. Of course, you have university in your future...*

Susan blinked back tears. These were early letters, and Rhys was tentative with his love. She could tell that he was concerned for her, even worried that he might cause an unwelcome disruption in her life. She remembered her impetuous response to this particular letter. She had told him that her future included him, that she loved him and wanted to return to Wales. From then on, his words were unencumbered. And so were hers.

> *Dearest Susan,*
>
> *You are constantly in my thoughts, always in my heart. It's hard for me to believe you love me—me, Rhys Llewellyn, a Welsh nobody. But I want to believe it. I do believe it! And I am the luckiest man on Earth! What great lyrics you quoted about dreaming—that old song sung by the Everly Brothers, "Whenever I want you, all I have to do is dream." My dreams are filled with you, my darling Susan!*

Susan's tears fell at the memory. Yes, she and Rhys dreamed. They dreamed through many more months of letters and declarations of love. Yet, in the end, their innocent dreams crumbled…replaced by reality. Reality wasn't nearly as sweet. She unfolded another letter.

> *My darling Susan,*
>
> *Because of you and your love, I have more energy and enthusiasm for my work than ever before. Not only am I putting funds aside, I'm also planning advertisements and seeking a smart location for my business. You said you fell in love with Wales (as well as with me!) while you were here. If you decide to make Wales your home, you'll find endless opportunities for your beautiful music. And, of course, there'll be me, one who loves you more than anyone else ever could.*

Susan had bravely responded:

> *…You said, if I decide to make Wales my home… Was that a hint, Rhys? Would you like me to make Wales my home? I can't think of any reason I would consider it, other than you. Do you love me that much? Are you thinking about marriage?*

And his letter came back:

> *Of course I've been thinking about marriage! But would I dare mention it straight out? You're so beautiful and talented, and you will have many wonderful opportunities to choose from. All I could do was hint and hope. And that's what I did. Would you even consider marrying me? ...I'm hoping...*

Susan always had hoped that she and Rhys would be together again someday. In fact, for the past year she'd been making plans to find him—without benefit of the Internet—but she had not yet confided in anyone. Not her sister Beth, nor Anwen, nor anyone else. She'd been saving money for a trip to Wales and was planning to go in the summer, just a few weeks away. She had decided to waste no more time worrying and wondering. No matter what lay ahead—even if the reality that had replaced Rhys's dreams was unbearably harsh, as hers had been— she was determined to look for him, to find him. To know. Not even Forrest Fletcher could stop her...but that was before she realized nineteen years had passed, and that devil was on his way out of prison. Could he stop her now? Would he try?

She pulled Rhys's last letter from the bottom of the stack, the message that had broken her heart.

> *This is my last letter, Susan. Something unfortunate has happened here, and I am leaving Snowdonia. You are beautiful and talented, and you deserve much more than I could ever give you. But please remember that I love you. We are soul mates, and I will love you <u>forever</u>.*

She, too, believed in soul mates and believed that she and Rhys were meant to be together. Whatever the circumstances, whatever had happened, it wouldn't be—*couldn't* be—enough to keep them apart. If Rhys truly meant it when he said he would love her forever—and she believed in her heart that he did—then he still loved her. She would find him; she would face him. And she would face his demons. And if, after all these years, there were no demons, if she found him happily married and content in life, she would smile and tell him that all she ever wanted was to know that he had found happiness. And it would be the truth. She was older, wiser, and stronger now.

She stood, straightening her shoulders. Her eyes no longer glistened with tears—they glistened with determination. Telling Annie about the locket and all it meant to her had been catharsis. Relief. It had helped her put her own desires in perspective. Whatever the outcome, she could handle it. She also could handle Forrest Fletcher and whatever meanness he might pursue. She would shove thoughts of that man right out of her head and straight to where they belonged—straight to hell! And she would tell Annie about her plan to revisit Wales!

~   ~   ~

"Hey, Mom!" Anwen called, stepping out onto the deck, suspending Susan's reverie. "I didn't find Rhys yet, but I did find something interesting on the Net—a newspaper account from July 1988 that mentions a Rhys Llewellyn and Snowdonia Tours in Conwy, Wales."

"Oh, let's go see!"

"Won't do you any good. It's in Welsh. What a messy language! No vowels. How can they pronounce that stuff?"

Susan laughed. "Welsh sounds as messy as it looks. We need to get it translated. Catrin's mother could do it, but she's back in Davenport, Georgia, and I haven't really been in touch with her for years."

"Surely there's someone at the university who can do it. I'm going out there in the morning to pick up some books I ordered. I'll check into it."

Susan's heart fluttered with excitement. *Rhys. . . . Maybe I'll learn what happened. Finally!* But she made herself a promise. No matter what she learned—no matter how terrible it was—it was in the past and she would still go to Wales. She would see him, face to face, one more time.

Anwen had tucked a printout into her pocket, out of sight. She did not want her mother to see the photo accompanying the article. Despite her excitement at finding news of Rhys, she had a tinge of concern about what the translation might reveal. The photo was worrisome. No, she would not show it to her mother. Rhys Llewellyn's sad, bewildered face would surely haunt Susan for the *next* twenty-one years.

Chapter 6
North Wales: 1988

Rhys had fallen in love with Susan exactly a year ago, but it seemed like an eternity. Since then, only letters back and forth across the ocean; and once, last Christmas, a brief phone call. No looking into her beautiful eyes, no listening to her exquisite music. No touching, no kisses. Now, he held her last letter in his hands. She'd sent a photo of herself and her sister, Beth, arms around each other, laughing. Happy. He swallowed hard, wanting to cry but much too old, a man at nineteen. He wouldn't be answering this letter or any others. There would be no further contact with Susan Evans, his first love, his only love. . . .*She's too good for me*, he thought. *Pretty, talented, with wealthy parents who will see to it she has an education. She doesn't need me and my troubles.* He held her letter to his lips and kissed it. *I'm going away, Susan. And I'm leaving no trace. . . because I love you so very much.*

He didn't consider that he was running; rather, he was "starting over." One day he'd been happy, excited about the future; and the next his world was in flames. Just that fast. An auditor had completed an examination of Snowdonia Tours' financial records and informed the owner of missing money, amounting to about 30,000 American dollars. Everyone knew about Rhys's big plans to have his own business someday. Many, including his friends, doubted he could ever raise the money; still, they had encouraged him. So as soon as the loss was discovered, tongues started flapping, and those who had encouraged Rhys quickly abandoned him, lest they be implicated in the trouble. Finally, the office manager, Mrs. Clougher (suitably pronounced "clucker"), deliberately pointed her chubby finger at Rhys as the person entrusted with bank deposits for the past year. That much was true. He had been given additional responsibilities, including some office work and the daily deposits. He had welcomed this, eager to learn all he could about the business before striking out on his own. But he did not steal the money.

"Always asking questions," Mrs. Clougher had said, accusation strong in her voice. "Wanting to know much more than was necessary."

"But...I thought you liked me," Rhys had said, disbelieving. "I thought you wanted to teach me."

"I did like you. That's what makes it so hard now, y' see. I was liking a thief!"

"I'm not a thief."

Still, there were discrepancies in the books, and bank slips had been altered. Rhys knew nothing about them, but he had no defense. Especially when Mrs. Clougher kept "clucking" out his opportunities. So he was taken into custody, and the article in the *Chronicle* was headed, "Snowdonia's Golden Boy Arrested." The accompanying photo was captioned, "Rhys Llewellyn."

Three months later the office manager, Mrs. Clougher herself, was caught in a small but critical lie. Under pressure, she confessed to the embezzlement, wailing, "'Twas only for me children and wee grandbabies!" and was sent to prison. A wily old woman, she was—didn't even *have* grandbabies. Rhys was exonerated, but three months of suspicion was long enough for him to lose faith in his so-called friends. That was when he learned he was truly alone in the world. Except for one person—another Arnhall orphan, named Brisen Devenallt, who lived in nearby Betws-y-Coed and commuted to her job at the woolen mill in Trefriw. She had been his best friend throughout childhood, a pretty little thing that the attendants at the orphanage had called "Snow White" because of her fair skin and black hair. Brisen remained his friend into adulthood and continued to stand by him during his ordeal. She called him every day with encouragement. And she met him during her lunch break at least twice a week, leaving Gavin— her live-in boyfriend who had no job—to fend for himself. Gavin didn't like to eat at the café in Trefriw anyway, and he didn't consider Rhys a threat.

"Y'd think I had the black plague," Rhys had said to her, while he was still under suspicion. "Everyone avoids me now—friends, co-workers, even Mr. Narberth who drove the van for me all those times."

"I know you didn't do it, Rhys. Please don't worry; the truth will come out," Brisen said. And she believed it.

"So what if it does? Who'd hire me now, with me mug all over North Wales?" His spoken dialect became more pronounced when he was angry.

"You don't need anyone to hire you, Rhys. You're going to start your own business, remember? So, when your innocence is proven and this is over, start it!"

"Oh, and who'll lend me the money then, after all the notoriety?"

"Mr. Whittal in Trefriw; that's who. The same person who offered it before. He's a kind and good man, Rhys, besides being very wealthy. You've already put aside your portion; you've proved yourself. And when your name is cleared, Mr. Whittal will be there for you. I know he will! He's always been there for the orphans of Arnhall."

"When my name is cleared! Cleared? That could be years from now!" But it was true about Siam Whittal. The man was a generous benefactor, himself having been an Arnhall orphan. He had known poverty, had known what it meant to struggle, earn, and profit. And he had profited very nicely indeed. In his late seventies now, he was committed not to handing out money to no purpose, but to helping others who wanted to work as he had worked.

Later, when Rhys had been declared innocent, Brisen reminded him of their conversation. They were having tea and pastry at the corner café in Trefriw.

"But I need to be employed a bit longer, Brisen," Rhys said. I need to show my strength of character before I go back to Mr. Whittal." He broke off a bit of pastry and swallowed it. "The owner of Snowdonia Tours has said my job is waiting for me, but I can't bear to return, knowing how they all shunned me. I don't even want to stay in Llandudno or work in Conwy. And I sure don't want to be on the dole!"

"You won't be! Not ever. Come home with me, Rhys," Brisen offered. "Come to Betws-y-Coed and stay with Gavin and me until you get it all figured out."

"Gavin won't mind?"

She shook her head. "He's not home much anyway. Come stay with us until you know what you want to do."

"Well, there's one thing I know right now I want to do."

"And what is that?"

"Change my name."

"What? You can't do that!"

"And why not? I've a perfectly good second name—Dafydd, after the patron saint of Wales." He smiled proudly. "Of course I'll spell it D-a-v-i-d. Easier for tourists to pronounce."

Brisen tried it out: "David Llewellyn. Hmmm. Not bad."

"Going to make that surname easier, too. L-e-w-e-l-l-e-n. Pronounced the same, but spelled differently. David Lewellen. Easier to say; easier to spell…and no connection to the old Rhys Llewellyn."

~   ~   ~

Two weeks later Rhys moved out of his rooms in Llandudno and into Brisen's tiny flat in Betws-y-Coed, just a short distance south of Trefriw. When he arrived with his few possessions, the flat looked strangely empty—no men's clothes on the floor; no beer bottles on the tea table. Brisen had tried always to keep things clean, but Gavin stayed a step ahead of her.

"How long has he been gone?" Rhys asked, emptying his suitcase into a cupboard she had allotted him. He would be sleeping on the sofa, which was just about long enough for his tall frame.

Brisen gave him a ghost of a smile. "You could tell?" she asked, tossing him a puffy pillow and a warm blanket.

"How long? Did he leave because of me?" Actually, Rhys and Gavin tolerated each other fairly well.

"No, not because of you. He was fine with that. It was…other stuff. He moved out two days ago." She sighed, her eyes turning sad.

"Are you sorry he's gone?"

"A little. He wanted to go south, to Cardiff, where there was some 'action,' as he called it. I didn't. Besides…he said he wanted to move on. He didn't want to get married."

"And you did?" Rhys's question was gentle.

Brisen nodded her head and blinked back tears. "I thought I loved him. Now I'm not so sure. Maybe I was just used to having him around. …Rhys—"

He interrupted her. "David. You must call me David now."

A tiny smile turned up one corner of her mouth. "David. …I hope you won't be too uncomfortable here."

He kissed her forehead. "Brisen, you're my sister, if not by blood then in spirit. I will never be uncomfortable with you. And thank you; thank you very much…for believing in me."

~   ~   ~

Experienced tour guides were welcomed in Betws-y-Coed, because tourists loved the town and swarmed over it all year round. It was centrally located to nearly all of Snowdonia National Park and had, since the dawn of the railway age, become a major resort with myriad accommodations. David Lewellen became a freelance guide, a very busy one. He traded his ten-year-old Mini on a used, six-passenger van, and Brisen co-signed the loan. When he got it tuned up and cleaned inside and out, it was more than adequate for squiring tourists around the area. In three months, he was ready to find a flat of his own and speak to Mr. Whittal about his offer to help finance a *real* tour company. However, Fate intervened and twisted his life into a pretzel once again.

Brisen was already home from her job in Trefriw when David returned from taking a group for a ride on the Blaenau-Ffestiniog Railway, a narrow-gauge steam train that offered a spectacular view of the mountains. He was exhilarated from the train tour, one of his favorites, and he was excited about finding his own place to live.

But as he started to tell Brisen the good news, his heart stopped. She was in tears. "What's wrong?" he asked. "Brisen, what is it?"

"I-I went…" More tears flowed. "Oh, David …It's Gavin. I can't, I can't!"

"Can't what?" David wrapped his arms around her. "Tell me, dear one. Why are you so upset?"

She dabbed at her eyes. *"Bum gall unwaith-hynny oedd, llefain pan ym ganed."*

"'I was wise once. When I was born, I cried.' …What are you trying to tell me, Brisen?"

"I haven't been very wise. Not wise at all. I-I went to the doctor today. …I'm going to have Gavin's baby, and I can't tell him. Even if I could find him, I can't! He would be very angry with me."

It was a stunning blow. "Have you heard from him since he left?"

"No. Not one word. He doesn't care for me at all, and he definitely would not want a baby. I can't tell him!"

"Do you want the baby?"

"David, you know I could never do anything to…to get rid of it. That would be horrible!" Brisen began crying anew.

David guided her to the sofa, pushing his blanket and pillow to the floor. "Here, sit down. Let's talk about this. I'll get you a cup of tea." He poured from the pot, which was steaming on the stove, and handed a cup to Brisen. "Drink," he commanded.

She sipped at the tea until her sniffling subsided. "What…what am I going to do?" she asked, more of herself than of David.

He had been thinking. After pouring himself some tea and taking several swallows, he said, "Let's get married."

"What? You can't be serious!"

"I am most definitely serious. You want the baby. You don't want Gavin. Your baby needs a name and a father. ...I'm here."

"You can't do this."

"Yes, I can. You stood up for me when no one else would. You took me in and kept my hope alive, Brisen. And I'm going to take care of you."

"But what about...what about Susan? I know how much you love her!"

He swallowed hard, fighting tears of his own. "I stopped writing to Susan when I was accused. She mustn't know about my troubles nor how alone I felt. ...I'll never see her again. She was a wonderful dream—one I'll never forget—but the dream is over."

"David, this is insane."

He put a finger over her lips. "No arguments. And one more thing, Brisen ...Please don't be concerned about my coming to your bed. I could not. I think of you only as my dearest friend and sister. When the time is right, you can divorce me and look for a true love. But know this—" He lifted his chin, and there was determination in his eyes and in his bearing. "I will say the child is mine, and I will always make sure you both are well cared for."

~   ~   ~

Two months later, Brisen received news of Gavin. He'd been working on a construction crew in Cardiff, renovating an old building. A support beam collapsed, trapping Gavin and one other worker beneath the wall. Gavin died instantly; the other man several hours after being rescued.

Brisen wept. She couldn't help it.

"I'm sorry, dear. Truly I am," David said, a comforting arm around her shoulders.

"It's not how you think, David. I'm over him." She dabbed at her eyes. "In fact, I don't believe that I ever really loved him. It's just...just that once upon a time I did care about him. I really did."

"Of course you did."

"I've been worrying lately, too. The closer I get to the baby's birth, the more guilty I've been feeling about not finding Gavin and telling him. Even though I knew he'd have been furious, I still was torn about his right to know. I thought he should be told—but I didn't want to tell him."

"I'm glad you didn't tell him." David pulled her head onto his shoulder. "I'm not being cruel, Brisen. I'm stating fact. With Gavin gone, there will never be a problem about parentage. You won't need to harbor feelings of guilt. And, as I told you when I asked you to marry me, I will say the child is mine. He or she need never know that I am not the biological father. …We're a family now."

Chapter 7

Anwen drove home from the university with the top down on her Mustang convertible, a graduation present from her grandfather. Her long golden hair was clipped up in back, but tendrils had escaped in the breeze and slapped at her face. She didn't notice. She should have been happy after having the Welsh article translated; she should have been happy taking news—any news at all of Rhys Llewellyn—to her mother. But the news was not good, and she was apprehensive.

Actually, it was a Welsh student who did the translation. When she asked at the bookstore, the manager directed her to the university library, where Brian Gruffydd worked part time. He was a tall, handsome young man with coppery hair and the greenest eyes Annie had ever seen.

"Your name is Anwen," he said, after she'd introduced herself. "You're Welsh! *Bore da! Sut wyt ti?*"

She laughed. "In name only. I don't understand a word of Welsh. In fact, that's why I've come to see you. I need something translated."

"My pleasure. There's a small conference room over there." He pointed. "Shall we?"

Anwen followed him to the windowed room overlooking the reference section. As they sat at the table, Brian asked, "Do you want me to read it to you, or would you be needing a printout?"

"A printout, please, if it's not too much trouble." She handed him the copy of the article she'd retrieved from the Internet.

"Easy to do." He pulled a computer keyboard toward him and said, "I'll enter the data as I read it." He glanced at the sheet. "From Llandudno, I see. Never been there, but I understand it's a nice place, lots of culture—art galleries, concerts, and the like. I'm from Swansea myself, down in the southern part of Wales."

47

As he began to read, Anwen forgot about his charming accent, and listened to the report with increasing anxiety. Rhys Llewellyn had been arrested for embezzling the equivalent of 30,000 American dollars from his employer. "The trusted employee," Brian read as he typed, "had access to the financial books and the deposit slips; and, according to the manager, Mrs. Clougher, was the only person with opportunity to make alterations." Brian looked up, speaking to Anwen. "Young, he was. Just nineteen. Were you…are you acquainted with him?" he asked.

Anwen shook her head. "No. He's someone my mother used to know. I was trying to find out what happened to him. But this doesn't look good, does it." It was a statement, not a question.

"This says only that he was arrested and granted bail." Brian said. "At this point he hadn't been tried. Do you have a follow-up article?"

"I guess I was so excited when I found this one that I stopped looking. But I can't just leave it like this. Mother will be devastated. They were very good friends," she added, lamely.

"Tell you what," Brian said. "I can find Welsh materials rather quickly—I know where to look—but I can't do it here or now. When I get back to my apartment—my last class ends at four o'clock—I'll fire up my PC and see what's out there on Mr. Llewellyn."

Anwen felt relief. "Oh, would you? I can pay for your time."

"Not necessary. Researching in Wales is pure fun for me. Just give me your e-mail address and I'll send you a note tonight." His eyes softened; and, suddenly less businesslike, he looked directly at her and asked, "…Are you a student here?"

"Almost. I'll start in September. Communication major."

"I'm a sophomore," he said. "I.T."

"Information Technology? I think I've come to the right person!"

There was a twinkle in his eye, as he held out his hand for her to shake. "Hope to see you around campus," he said.

Anwen flashed him a brilliant smile, thinking, *That would be very nice!*

~   ~   ~

"That news report is absurd, Annie! I realize that I was with him for only ten days, but we did write back and forth for an entire year after that. I knew him. He wasn't the kind of person to steal. Rhys was proud of what he'd accomplished on his own. He was eager to start his business. He would never have jeopardized what he'd worked so hard for!" Susan put the translation sheet down. She and Anwen were seated at the kitchen table, drinking coffee. The sandwiches Annie had made remained untouched.

"Brian is looking for follow-up information. He said he would e-mail tonight and let me know what he finds."

"If Rhys has been in prison all these years for something he didn't do, I'll…I'll never forgive myself for…for—"

"For what, Mom? You didn't do anything wrong."

"I didn't do anything at all! That's what bothers me." New tears formed.

"How could you? You were a young teenager. You didn't know. But let's not get ahead of ourselves here. Maybe Brian can turn up good news. There could be a simple explanation for this." *Or maybe he died all those years ago,* Anwen thought, sadly.

Susan sighed. "Even so, Rhys must have gone through hell and back with this terrible accusation hanging over him. …I'm not hopeful, Annie. I believe if he could have written to me, he would have." *Now I'm more anxious than ever to go to Wales,* Susan thought. *I'm going to find him!*

"Rhys could have been embarrassed by all of this," Anwen said. "It's possible that he didn't want to trouble you with it. He was the same age then as I am now. Putting myself in his place, I'd probably do exactly that—I'd back off so that my boyfriend wouldn't be burdened with my problems. …If I were really in love, that is. And, Mom, after reading some of the letters you shared with me last night, I'd say that boy was in love. *Really* in love."

Anwen pushed the plate of sandwiches toward her mother. "Eat!" she commanded, smiling. She chose a sandwich for herself and took a bite, washing it down with iced tea. "We had planned to go shopping this afternoon, so let's do it. I need new clothes for school, and shopping will take your mind off Rhys for a little while. Let's think positive. Let's believe that tonight Brian will have good news for us."

And maybe tonight, Susan thought, *I'll tell Annie about my plan to go to Wales.*

~ ~ ~

They spent the afternoon at Governor's Square Mall trying on clothes; and Susan's sister, Beth, joined them for dinner at Anthony's Italian Restaurant across town. Susan's mood was somewhat relieved, but Rhys still wasn't far from her mind, always in her heart.

Beth, who'd known about Rhys since the beginning, was disturbed by the newspaper article and spoke firmly, though lovingly, to Susan. "If this turns out to be a prison story, Susan," she said, "you don't need any part of it. You've already been through a prison ordeal with Fletch."

"How can you even think of comparing those two men?" Susan asked. "Fletcher was—is—a criminal, a pervert!"

"That reminds me, isn't he scheduled for—"

"No way! No way can you compare him to Rhys!" Susan had purposely cut Beth off before she could mention Forrest Fletcher's looming freedom. She also gave her sister a look that said, *Don't go there.* "Rhys was never anything but good, kind, honest…"

"You hope he was honest, Sis, but be ready to deal with your feelings if the news comes back that he was guilty."

"He wasn't guilty! I know he wasn't."

"I'm just saying, be prepared."

Susan loved her older sister dearly. Beth and her husband, Joel Montgomery, a pediatrician with a growing practice and a kind heart, had taken her into the guest quarters of their lovely home when she was pregnant with Annie. This enabled Susan to leave wagging tongues behind in Davenport, Georgia, and start a new life in Tallahassee where her parents visited often. The Montgomery's daughter, Marlena, was eighteen months old at the time, and Marlena and Annie grew up as close as sisters. When Annie was six months old, Susan began classes at Florida State, working on her Bachelor of Music in Guitar Performance, and Annie and Marlena shared a nanny in the Montgomery household. Later, after Annie started kindergarten, Susan earned a master's degree.

So, despite her ordeal with Forrest Fletcher, Susan Evans had lived a privileged life. She now taught classical guitar part-time in the same university where she had perfected her craft. And, she had worked very hard over the years to become a concert performer, though she was a long way from being famous. Her determination had always been fired by memories of Rhys and the look in his eyes when he talked of owning his own company. His life had not been privileged. He'd grown up in an orphanage and struggled with his dreams of the future. *With my opportunities,* Susan had thought just after Annie's birth, *how can I do less? I owe it to Rhys, and to myself, to hold my head high—far above the Forrest Fletchers of this world—and become the best musician I can possibly be. …*And she had.

"Okay," Susan said to Beth. "I'll prepare myself for any news about Rhys. If I remember correctly, that's exactly what you said to me twenty years ago. You didn't believe I was in love then, Beth."

Beth sighed. "I was six years older than you, no longer a teenager, and I was thinking of my own teen years, when everything was bigger than life, more important, more *real* than anything anyone else could possibly experience. That's where I was coming from. I supposed you'd had an interesting little fling in a foreign country—a fairy tale romance with a knight in shining armor and all that goes with it—and I was certain you'd get over it in time. I treated your love for Rhys as insignificant…and I'm very sorry." She leaned over and gave her sister a hug. "I'm here for you," she said. "I'll always be here for you."

Susan smiled and expressed her gratitude. "Thank you. I'm glad I have both you and Annie in my corner, because I'm going to need you. I assure you, I will do *something* with the information once we get it. I won't just sit around for another two decades wishing things were different!"

Beth raised her wine glass. "To the new Susan," she said, "and to us—the Three Musketeers. We're sticking together!"

~　~　~

Brian's e-mail arrived just after nine o'clock:

I found what you were looking for, Anwen. There are two articles. The first is a report in The Evening Ledger, dated Friday, August 12, 1988. The heading is: Snowdonia's Golden Boy Still Golden. Here's my translation:

Early yesterday afternoon Mrs. Andras Clougher was confronted by investigators and admitted to embezzling funds from Snowdonia Tours of Conwy. Office manager for three years past, Mrs. Clougher's theft had taken place gradually over twenty-two months. Her arrest removes all suspicion from Rhys Llewellyn, who had previously been charged, based primarily on Mrs. Clougher's testimony. Often referred to as "Snowdonia's Golden Boy," Llewellyn had endeared himself to locals and tourists alike, with his winning personality and vast knowledge of the Snowdonia area. When asked about his plans for the future, Llewellyn had no comment.

Anwen, the second article comes from The Pioneer, a free weekly that circulates in the Colwyn Bay area, which covers a good portion of the North Wales coast. This one, a Letter to the Editor, is a bit more chatty:

After six weeks of finger-pointing and speculation, our own Rhys Llewellyn has been cleared of the crime of embezzlement. It's about time! Young Llewellyn is a hard-working citizen, devoted to his chosen career and beloved by all who know him. As one of his former co-workers, I regret that Llewellyn suffered such injustice at another's hand, especially that of a so-called supervisor. Also, I'm sorry that I (and others like me) did not offer support and friendship to Rhys in his time of trouble, as we should have. We all were afraid for our jobs. I wish him well, and I hope as he moves forward that he never looks back!

I do wish I could have found more, but it just isn't there to find. It's like Rhys Llewellyn dropped off the face of the earth, or at least left the area sometime in August 1988. For what it's worth, he's not listed in any obituaries. Anwen, feel free to give me a call if you'd like to discuss this. Or, just give me a call. :)

Anwen smiled to herself, thinking, *Thanks for the excuse, Brian. I certainly will give you a call!*

Chapter 8
London, England: The Present

David Lewellen stood at his office window, looking down on Norfolk Square, so pretty in spring. Carefully tended beds of flowers waved their colorful petals beneath the trees, and here and there a bird hopped along one of the walkways. He loved this area of London—Paddington, his home for the past eighteen years, though he had to admit the neighborhood was slowly changing, not necessarily for the better. He and Brisen had moved here shortly after Nia's birth.

Two quick taps on the office door, then it opened. "Dad? Can I clear that van trip we talked about this morning? The one to Cambridge? It's going to be an overnight."

He turned to look at his beautiful daughter—long, black hair just like Brisen's, and her mother's beautiful smile. He was glad she looked like Brisen rather than Gavin; that meant there would never be a question about her not being David Lewellen's natural daughter.

"Sure," he said, "as long as Nigel is available to guide it. He's the only one who knows that city's thirty-some colleges one from the other. Oh, are the travelers American?"

"Yes, from Virginia."

"Then be sure to include the Cambridge American Cemetery on the tour. ...You know the routine, Nia," he added with a smile.

She gave him a "thumbs up" and backed out, closing the door.

Nia had been working for All England Tours, David's company, for the past year and was a welcome addition to his staff. She had a genuine gift for the business and loved interacting with tourists. They, in turn, appreciated her interest in their needs, her knowledge of the country, and her youthful sense of humor.

"Please, Dad," she had begged a year ago. "I've been hanging about here since I was in nappies. It's what I want to do. I can go to university later."

So he and Brisen relented. So far, it had been a good decision.

David and Brisen were still great friends, though they'd been divorced for seventeen years, a marriage never consummated. Brisen had met and married Kent Crowther, the love of her life, and she and David had shared custody of Nia during the child's growing-up years. Brisen, with a talent for lettering, had taken a course in calligraphy and now managed a sign shop on nearby Praed Street. She often stopped by the tour office for a chat.

David, however, had not remarried. He'd had a few relationships, the longest lasting a mere eight months. He'd never been able to forget Susan Evans, the girl whose photograph he now held in his hands. Years ago he'd had a couple of copies made of the snapshot her friend had taken at the Great Orme—of the two of them together. One photo was on his nightstand at home. The other fit nicely in his wallet.

In his flat in Sussex Gardens were several more pictures of Susan, photos he'd downloaded from the Internet, printed, and framed. He'd "found" his first love ten years before—though she never knew—while leafing through an American magazine at a London bookshop. The sight of her beautiful silhouette nearly stopped his heart. She was easy to recognize. Still looked sixteen, cradling her guitar in her arms, her head bent forward, silky blond hair shimmering over her shoulders. He bought the magazine and continued to follow her career over the years, watching her emerge as a sought-after classical guitarist, reading of her guest appearances with the Tallahassee Symphony, the Tampa Bay Symphony, and other community orchestras. He imagined she must be very happy with such a glamorous and fulfilling life. She was in her element, doing exactly what she was meant to do, though he wished it had worked out a bit differently, with her as a performer in Great Britain. With her as his wife.

Just then his secretary rang, informing him that Brisen had arrived. He closed his wallet and was putting it in his pocket as she entered the office.

"Looking at Susan again?" she asked, gently.

He smiled. "Always."

"David, why don't you contact her? It's been more than twenty years. What are you waiting for?"

He shrugged, sinking into one of the two comfy chairs in front of the window. "I doubt she'd remember me."

Brisen quickly crossed the room and sat beside him. "David, I don't often try to tell you what to do, but—"

He interrupted her, managing a quick laugh. "You never try."

"Well, I am now! Do you want to waste the next twenty years, just thinking about her? Dreaming, wondering? You know from reading press releases that she's single. Maybe she's pining for you the same as you are for her!

"Pining?" he teased.

"You know what I mean—longing, desiring, aching—and don't deny you feel those things."

"Oh, I'll not deny that. But Susan having those feelings for me? No, Brisen. She's almost famous, will be, within a few years. She has everything. Why would she give me a thought?"

"Just consider the possibility that she still loves you. What if she's been trying to find you? You haven't made it easy for her, leaving Wales, changing your name...getting married."

He turned his head sharply toward her. "I'll never regret marrying you. I love you as a dear sister. And I love Nia—she's my daughter as much as if I'd fathered her....More! And she'll never know otherwise. I'm very grateful to you, Brisen, for allowing me to be Nia's father."

"And I am deeply grateful for your loving deception." She took his hand in hers. "That's not why I mentioned our marriage just now. Nia has always understood that you and I are great friends but not destined to be lovers. I was so lucky to find Kent and to be able to tell him the truth about you and me and Nia. I love him more than I ever thought possible to love another human being; in that way, that is. I want the same for you, David. Don't you see? Our family isn't complete. Kent, me, Nia, you—we're out of balance. You need a woman to love," she added softly.

"I've tried..."

"But none of them was right for you. You need Susan." She released his hand and stood. "Contact her. I *am* telling you what to do." She turned to leave. "Do it!"

~　　~　　~

At closing time Nia bounced into David's office and plopped into a chair, stretching her long legs out in front of her.

"The Cambridge tour is all set," she said, "and we've a group of eight leaving for the Lake District tomorrow. Also tomorrow, Trudy is taking two Canadian couples to Bath; they specifically want to see the Roman spa and underground ruins. And, on Wednesday night I'm taking six young Japanese men on a pub crawl."

Her father turned a stern eye toward her.

"Just kidding, Dad!" Nia laughed aloud. "Not a bad idea though."

"It's a very bad idea." He grinned. "You'd scare them so much they'd never want to return to England."

"So what are you doing tonight?" she asked.

David shrugged. "Some reading, I guess.

"I have a better plan. Mrs. Clawson gave me two tickets to *Phantom of the Opera* at Her Majesty's Theatre, and I don't have a date."

"Why'd she give you tickets?"

"A last-minute thing. Someone gave them to her and she couldn't go." She jumped up and grabbed his hand. "Come on, take me out to dinner, and I'll take you to the theater."

"But I've seen *Phantom*."

"So have I, twice. But it's always fun. And you can't say you have anything better to do."

He smiled broadly. "No, I can't. I shall never have anything better to do than be with my lovely daughter. Let's go!"

~   ~   ~

"How can you drink that stuff, Dad?" Nia pointed to David's pint of Guinness, very dark with a creamy head. "Looks like tar. Tastes like it too."

David laughed. "You've tasted tar, m'dear?" They were relaxing after the show in a fairly quiet pub on Haymarket. "I really did enjoy *Phantom* once again," he said. "Thanks for taking me."

"No problem. . . .Oops! I mean, 'you're welcome.' I know you despise that American expression." She lifted her Newcastle brown ale toward her father. "Anyway, you're a fun date," she said. "You should go out more. With women your own age. You need a girlfriend."

"Why? I'm happy with things the way they are."

"Why? Because in a few months you'll be forty years old. *Forty*, Dad."

"Forty's not old."

Nia rolled her eyes. "To me it is. You can't stay single all your life."

"Hey, can we change the subject?" David finished his beer and motioned for another. "I started drinking Guinness while I was still in Wales. Welsh beer, you know, is notoriously mild. My friends and I thought the Irish imports had a lot more punch."

"No kidding. And, no, we cannot change the subject. Dad, you're a great catch—handsome, intelligent, rich, fun to be with, and for a few months yet, still young."

He laughed. "I liked it all but the last point."

"Well, *my* point is that you're lonely and you don't need to be."

"Nia, I'm too busy to be lonely."

"Yes, you're busy, but I think you stay that way so you won't have to be alone." She reached across the table and placed her hand over his. "Dad, I have to tell you something."

"Oh, my god. Are you getting married?"

"Of course not! Mick and I are just good friends. For now. What I have to tell you is that Mum and I had a talk the other day. About you."

"…And?"

"And she told me about Susan." David started to object, but Nia pressed on. "I've known for a long time that you and Mum were great friends who needed each other, but weren't really in love the way people should be if they intend to spend the rest of their lives together. But I never knew about your love for Susan. Mum said it was very special and that you have a picture of her in your wallet. …May I see it?" Again, David started to object. "Please?" she asked.

Reluctantly, he took the wallet out of his pocket, removed the photo and handed it to his daughter.

"Oooh…." Nia's face lit up. "The two of you don't look much younger than I am right now."

"I was your age. Susan was two years younger."

Nia concentrated on the photo. "Susan is very pretty, blond, sweet-looking. And her eyes…the way she looks at you. And yours… It's easy to see that you loved each other." She glanced up at her father, and he looked away. "Dad, I think your story is the most beautiful, most…" She took a big breath and released it quickly. "It's the saddest story I've ever heard!" Her eyes began to mist as she returned the photo to him. "It's sad because it isn't finished. And it never will be finished unless you contact her. …Don't shake your head back and forth!"

"Nia, all those years ago I let her down. I didn't want Susan to know about the trouble I was in. You know—what happened in Wales, why I came here. I didn't want her to know about it, even though it wasn't my fault. She was so much…so much more than I was—headed for university and an exciting career. I was nothing. A nobody."

"But look at yourself now: You've built a business that earns more than you can spend in a lifetime, and it was your hard work that accomplished it. I'm proud of you; Mum's proud of you, and Susan would be proud of you, too…if she knew."

David's insides were churning. He didn't want to talk about Susan. "Nia, why are you trying to spoil a perfectly wonderful evening?"

"I'm trying to make it better. Truly, I am."

"Earlier today your mother was going on about it, too. Are you ladies conspiring against me?"

Nia smiled. "Yes, we've been talking, but not against you—for you. Would you just *think* about contacting her? Please?"

He never could resist his daughter's big dark eyes, and now that they were filled with such youthful hope and sincerity…well, yes, he could think about it. Truth is, he'd been thinking about it for quite a while. In fact, he'd even traveled the Internet in search of Susan Evans and found her address and phone number; but he needed someone with more technical expertise to track her e-mail address. Maybe his secretary?

"What if I found her e-mail address for you?" Nia asked. "Would you send her a note?"

"Huh?"

"I said—"

"I heard what you said, dear." He spoke gently. "That would be a very nice thing for you to do. … Yes, if you find her e-mail address, I'll *think* about sending a message."

Again, Nia reached across the table and squeezed his hand. "Thanks, Dad." She smiled. "At times like this, you make me feel like a real grownup."

Chapter 9

"Brian Gruffydd, please," Anwen said to the male voice on the other end of the line. She knew that Brian pronounced his last name *Griffith*.

"Sure. Hang on." The receiver was cupped, and Anwen heard a muffled, "Hey, Brian! This must be the call you were expecting. Smoooth voice!"

Brian grabbed the phone. "Hello!"

"You were expecting my call?" Anwen asked with a chuckle.

"My roommate is nosy. You do have a smooth voice, though."

She could tell he was smiling. "Thanks. I hope I'm not calling too late."

"Are you kidding? I'll be studying for at least two more hours. So, did you like those news reports better than the first one?"

"Yes! Thank you so much, Brian. I haven't shown them to Mom yet; I wanted to call you first and say Thanks. This means a lot to me, and it will make a big difference in Mom's life. She's been agonizing over Rhys's disappearance for years. Of course we still don't know where he is, but at least we know that he was cleared of that awful charge."

"Are you going to search for him?"

"Definitely. ...I probably shouldn't tell you why...but maybe you'll have some ideas that could help the search, with your knowledge of Wales and all."

"Tell me whatever you want to; I'll keep it confidential; and I'll help in any way I can, Anwen. I mean that."

She took a deep breath. "Well, Rhys Llewellyn is Mom's 'lost love.' They met in Wales twenty-one years ago, fell in love, corresponded for about a year; then he disappeared. He wrote a very sad last letter, which I now know was related to the theft he was accused of. What I don't understand is why he didn't contact her after he was exonerated."

"He was probably ashamed that he'd even been *considered* untrustworthy. We

Welsh are a proud lot, and I can understand his reluctance. For us, there's no going back. I've no doubt he moved out of the area to get a new start, maybe to South Wales, where I came from."

"According to Mom, his great ambition was to own a tour company; and, at the time of the theft, he was working to save money, which a benefactor had promised to match. Mom said he was very smart and determined and had even completed his business plan. ...It's just so sad."

"Maybe we should start looking at tour companies in the U.K. and see if he turns up."

"What a great idea! ...I did notice you said *we*."

"I certainly did. Should we discuss it over dinner tomorrow night?"

Anwen smiled into the phone, unable—and unwilling—to mask her excitement. "Absolutely!" she said.

And they made plans.

~   ~   ~

Susan was curled up on a sofa in the living room, with a cup of hot tea and the latest novel by her favorite "escape" author, Janet Evanovich. She was laughing aloud at the preposterous situation the characters were in, when Anwen entered the room.

"Must be a good book," Annie said.

"Yes, and I needed a good laugh!" Susan said, still chuckling. "These books never fail to take me away from reality and into something ridiculously fun."

"Well, you can keep right on smiling, because I have good news about Rhys." She offered the printout and Susan grabbed it.

"Really?" The book was forgotten, as she quickly read Brian's translations of the news articles. She finished with a sigh of relief. "I knew it! I knew he couldn't have taken the money. He was honest, sweet, sincere..." She looked at her daughter. "He was everything good." She turned her attention back to the reports. "But it doesn't say anything about where Rhys went afterward. Your friend, Brian, says he disappeared. What could have happened after this?"

"Brian has promised to help us look for him. In fact..." She paused and smiled. "I'm having dinner with him tomorrow evening."

"Annie, that's wonderful! You need to go out more; and from what you've told me, Brian seems very nice."

"Yeah. He is. But we're going to keep our minds focused on solving your mystery. For now, anyway." She sat down beside her mother and squeezed her hand.

"I love you, Annie," Susan said. "...Don't ever forget it." Her last sentence had special poignancy, as once again the soon-to-be-released Forrest Fletcher cast a shadow on her happiness. She wanted her love to always support and sustain Anwen, because she had no doubt Fletch would make his presence known, despite the order never to contact his victims. Soon she must warn Annie. Soon.

Now, however, she wanted to concentrate on positive things. On Rhys. This seemed like the right time to tell Annie about her plan to return to Wales. And, another idea had just struck her.

"My teaching schedule ends in two weeks," she began, "followed by my concert with the Tallahassee Symphony. Then..."

"Then what?"

"Then my calendar is clear. You'll have a couple of months before you move out and start college. Maybe we could do something special together before things get hectic again." She shrugged. "Like maybe take a little trip."

Annie's eyebrows shot up and she smiled. "That's a coy look on your face, Mom. Are you thinking what I think you're thinking?"

Susan shrugged again, her eyes bright.

"Like maybe a little trip to *Wales*?" Annie asked.

"...Well?"

"Wow! I'd love it! And we could find Rhys, and..."

"And even if we don't, I need to try. I *need* to, Annie."

"Mom, what if we find him and he doesn't want to talk to you?"

"That would be very sad; but, either way, I need to know. I need to fill the empty space that was Rhys. ...Otherwise, I will always feel that my life has been incomplete."

"Then we'll give it our best shot." Anwen jumped up and headed for the bookshelves across the room. "The atlas!" she explained. "I want to see a map of Wales. You can show me where we're going." Her sudden enthusiasm lit up the room and enveloped Susan, who felt happier than she'd been in a very long time.

They sat together, the map opened between them, and Susan pointed to the northern coast.

"There's Llandudno, where the festival was held—" She broke off suddenly, looking up. "...Oh, Annie, I just thought of something! The festival is always held during the first part of July. It's possible we'll be there while it's happening! Let's go online and find out!" She started up but Annie grabbed her hand and tugged, laughing.

"Hold on there, Mom. First you're going to show me Wales on this map. *Then* we'll go online."

Susan fell back onto the sofa, a bright smile covering her whole face. "I'm so excited! I can't believe this is happening. Annie, dear, you're a gem!"

"So where will we be going?" Annie put the atlas back on her mother's lap.

"Well, here…" Susan moved her finger slightly southwest of Llandudno but still on the coast, "is Conwy, where Rhys's employer was headquartered. Oh, Annie, that's such a quaint little town, and it's protected by a castle and rock walls all around."

"A castle!"

"Not like those in fairy tales. This castle was built hundreds of years ago. Now, it's just a fascinating ruin."

"I can't imagine actually being in a castle, ruin or not!"

"In a few weeks you'll get your chance. There are medieval castles all over Wales," Susan said. "I know because we students had to study Welsh history before the trip. Our chaperones, the Fleetwoods, insisted; and I've remembered most of it because…well, because Wales has remained so dear to my heart." She swallowed hard, then continued the geography and history lesson, pointing out Bodnant Garden and Trefriw further south. "That's where Catrin Fenna's grandparents lived. They died several years ago, just a few months apart. I don't suppose there's any of her family left there now. Trefriw is also where Rhys and I had our first kiss."

"We'll find him, Mom," Anwen promised. "Brian and I are going to work very hard on it in the next few weeks. I'll bet we locate Rhys before the—what shall we call it? Our vacation?"

"Yes! Our vacation. Together." Susan hugged her daughter. "Oh, Annie, thank you for being so understanding. Thank you for being you!"

Annie closed the atlas. "*Now* we'll go online," she said.

~   ~   ~

The next evening Brian took Anwen to a Japanese steak house, where they watched the chef put on a fine show—dicing, stirring, flipping, and purposely setting their food on fire. They laughed and ate and laughed some more. When they talked, it was mostly about FSU, Brian's experiences there, and what Anwen could expect when she started classes in the fall.

"What brought you all the way from Wales to FSU?" Anwen asked.

"My big brother. Well, sort of. He—Gareth—is five years older, a great soccer player. He was recruited to play soccer for Thomas University, just north of here in Georgia. A great opportunity for him. When he was a junior, I came to visit, thinking I might go there too—he really liked it—but we drove to Tallahassee one day and met some guys from FSU, took the tour, and…well, I knew this was the place for me. What about you? Why didn't you choose somewhere far from home?"

"I like it here. It's familiar—my mother's alma mater."

"Commuting from home, Anwen?"

"Nope. I'll be on campus."

"Hmmm." Brian's eyes sparkled.

As they left the restaurant, Anwen linked her arm in his and said, "You could call me Annie, you know, or Ann."

Brian flashed the smile she had so quickly come to love. "Ah, no," he said. "To me—*for* me—you will always be Anwen, and for very good reason. Do you know what your name means in Welsh?"

She shook her head. "No, and I doubt Mom knows either. She picked it out of a book of Welsh names because she liked the way it looked when she wrote it on paper."

They stopped at the car and Brian opened the door for her. "Your name means 'very beautiful,' and that's exactly what you are," he said.

Anwen's breath caught in her throat, but she managed to say, "Until I met you, I'd never heard my name spoken with a Welsh accent. I like it."

Brian laughed. "And that's why I can never call you Annie or Ann. I like the way *Anoowen* rolls off my tongue."

She turned her face up to his and he kissed her…lightly, sweetly…lingering. "*Anoowen*," he said.

As they turned onto Thomasville Road, Anwen told him about the planned trip to Wales.

"Ah, you'll love my country," he said. "Steep valleys, sharp ridges—a rugged landscape, very impressive. Also, it's very clean, no smoke or grime. Utterly peaceful."

"Mom said essentially the same thing. She said the peace of Wales never left her and still sustains her during the lonely times." Anwen shook her head. "Mom has loved and missed Rhys Llewellyn all of her life."

"Forgive me for asking, but…is Mr. Llewellyn your father? Is that why your mom wants to see him again?"

"No. It's been twenty-one years since she saw him. I'm only eighteen. My, uh…the man who fathered me…is someone I've never met." She shuddered, lowering her head. "And I never want to."

"It's okay." He put a finger to his lips. "I'm sorry I mentioned it. You don't have to say any more." He reached across the console to squeeze her hand, then changed the subject. "Too bad I can't go with you to Wales—to be your guide, I mean. Summer school, you know, and I'm committed to working in the library to help pay my fees."

"A guide would be nice, but we'll be fine. Oh, as it turns out, the annual festival in Llandudno, which Mom attended so many years ago, will be happening again this year during the time we're there. Part of the time anyway."

"Splendid!"

"She's excited about it, but we won't hang around the festival much. Too busy looking for Rhys. Got to keep our sights on the goal."

"So, what are your travel plans? Flights, I mean."

"We're flying to Dublin and taking the ferry across, then renting a car. That seemed the easiest way to go, since there isn't a large airport nearby. We prefer a long ferry ride to an extra-long train ride from England or South Wales. I've never been on one of those big ferries," she added.

"Just like a cruise ship, they are. You'll enjoy it. …So what would you like to do now? It's still quite early."

They glanced at each other and started laughing, as both had the same thought, *Your place or mine?*

"If I remember right," Anwen said, tucking a long blond wisp of hair behind her ear, "the purpose of this, uh, dinner meeting, was to discuss finding Rhys Llewellyn."

"We got sidetracked."

"So, how about I watch you follow clues on the Internet. Would you mind terribly?"

"My place it is!" he said with a grin.

Chapter 10

After two hours of Internet searching, midnight had come and gone, and Brian and Anwen were both weary. They'd concentrated on tour companies—first those based in Wales, then others with the broader base of the United Kingdom.

"We've tried everything from Back-Roads Touring to Undiscovered Britain," Anwen said, standing and stretching, "and not one Rhys Llewellyn."

Brian logged off his computer. "Early this morning I extended the personal searches, too. Found no Rhys Llewellyns that matched—just some that were way off the mark, including a fourteen-year-old hacker in Peterborough and a Scotsman of sixty-two who's looking for 'companionship.'"

Anwen laughed. "There were a couple of Lewellens—wrong spelling—listed with tour companies but still no Rhys. Only an Owen and a David."

"Maybe our Mr. Llewellyn has changed his name to something different altogether."

"Oh, no! I hadn't thought of that. Maybe he did exactly that because of all the trouble he went through. If that's the case, we'll never find him. Can you think of anything else we can do, Brian?"

He stood, putting his hands on her shoulders. "You and your mom are already doing it. You're going to Wales. The only way to find this man is to find someone who knows him, or at least someone who knows where he went."

Anwen leaned into his arms. "Thank you, Brian," she said. "Thank you for all your help. I do wish you could go with us."

"Me, too. But I'll be here when you get back. . . . And not just to hear about Rhys Llewellyn." He put his hand beneath her chin and lifted her face. "I want to hear about you. All about you."

He kissed her, and she trembled—just a little, but enough to betray her feelings for him.

She took a deep breath and pushed away with a smile. "I noticed that your roommate—what is his name?"

"Ramsey."

"Yeah. Ramsey is conveniently absent."

Brian said nothing but looked at her, imploringly.

She shook her head and reached for her shoulder bag. "This isn't the time, Brian."

"Maybe sometime?"

"Maybe."

~   ~   ~

Two weeks later the plans were nearly complete. Susan and Anwen had packed and unpacked several times, trying to fit their belongings into small backpacks. They had decided to travel very light, a backpack and shoulder pack for each of them—simple, easy, hands-free, and no worrying about lost luggage.

Annie tapped on her mother's bedroom door.

"Come in," Susan called, stepping into the room from the adjoining bathroom.

Anwen opened the door and stopped, staring. "...What in the world are you doing?" she asked, finally, not knowing whether to laugh or scream. Above each of Susan's beautiful eyes was a thick, gooey, dark brown line. "You look like Groucho Marx!" Annie cried.

Susan peered into her dressing-table mirror. "You think so?"

Annie moved closer. "I know so. What is that stuff?"

"I'm dying my eyebrows. Don't worry; they'll turn out light brown, just right to go with my blond hair. It covers the gray."

Annie burst out laughing. "Why? You don't have gray eyebrows."

"Of course not," Susan said, suppressing a grin. "I don't have gray hair either." Annie rolled her eyes and it was Susan's turn to laugh. "Time to wash this off," she said. "It's only supposed to stay on for five minutes." She headed back toward the bathroom. "You wanted something?"

"Yeah, Groucho. I picked up our plane tickets and booked us a room at the Clarence Hotel in Llandudno."

Susan's breath caught in her throat. "Is it really happening, Annie?" She grabbed her daughter's arm. "Do you think we'll find him?"

"Of course we will. But you'd better get that godawful stuff off your face or you'll be greeting him *without* eyebrows!"

~ ~ ~

The next night was Susan's solo appearance with the Tallahassee Symphony, the only thing of importance remaining before leaving for Wales. Spring session had ended at the university, and Ruby Diamond Auditorium was sold out for the concert.

As Anwen and Brian ascended the venue's wide front steps on Saturday night, Brian said, "I'm impressed. Really, I am."

"With what? You've been here before."

"Of course I have, silly. I mean I'm impressed with your mom."

"Lots of people are. She's very talented."

"That's not what I mean."

They stopped inside the lobby and she turned to face him. "So what do you mean?"

"C'mon. I knew your name was Evans and your mother was Susan, but I never put it together until tonight. Your mother is *the* Susan Evans, and you didn't tell me! Nor did she tell me, when we went to dinner with her the other night. She's famous!"

Anwen laughed. "Only in a limited area of the Southeast, though she deserves much more." She pulled the tickets out of her purse and handed them to Brian. "Compliments of Mom. Our tickets are next to the Montgomerys—my Aunt Beth and Uncle Joel."

"Hey, thanks for inviting me and for letting me meet more of your family."

"After tonight, the only family you won't have met are my grandparents and my cousin, Marlena. Very small crew."

Brian put his arm around her waist and gave her a little hug as he presented their tickets to the usher. Beth and Joel were already seated. Anwen made the introductions and sat next to Beth.

"I hear you're going to Wales," Beth said into her niece's ear, adding, "I hope it's not a fool's errand."

"We're leaving tomorrow afternoon, and even if we don't find Rhys, we're going to have a great time together. I've never been on a long trip with Mom, and I'm really looking forward to it."

"I wish you both the best of luck, Annie; I really do. I must say, Sis hasn't looked this happy in years. Even her music couldn't put the glow on her face that I've seen lately. . . . By the way," she continued in a whisper, "you've got a kind of glow, too. Is Brian causing it?"

Just then the lights dimmed and Anwen was spared answering, though she couldn't help the big smile that enveloped her face.

The varied program included Mendelssohn's "Song Without Words" and a Scarlatti sonata. On the lighter side was "All I Ask of You" from *Phantom of the Opera*. Time passed very quickly and soon they were outside under the lamps, heading toward the parking lot. Susan had remained behind in the auditorium with her fellow musicians.

"She was absolutely magnificent," Brian said. "I've heard plenty of good musicians, not only in Wales but also here at Florida State, but…you know, there's something that sets her apart. Something special. I can't quite put my finger on it."

"I know what it is," Beth offered. "It's *feeling*. She feels every note she plays. I asked her about that very thing many years ago, and she told me that once her fingers knew which strings to play and when, then she didn't have to think any more about what she was doing, only how she *felt* about it. She masters the technique, then loses herself in the music."

"That's it. That's definitely it. Are you musical too, Beth?" he asked.

"Hah! Only in the shower."

"An off-key canary," Joel offered, grinning. "That's my Beth." He gave his wife a hug. "Say, Brian, how'd you like that *Phantom* piece Susan played tonight?"

"Wonderful! I saw *Phantom of the Opera* in London a couple of years ago."

"Really? I've never been to London," Annie said, "but I'd love to go someday."

"Well, that show's been lighting up Her Majesty's stage for more than twenty years and will no doubt be there for many more."

Beth joined in. "Hey, Annie, why don't you and Susan just dip on over to London from Wales?" Anwen shook her head. "I'm serious," Beth said. "You'll only be a few hours from there. What a great opportunity!"

"Can't think about that right now. We've got to stay focused on the goal, and the goal is Rhys Llewellyn."

"Stick with it, Annie," her Uncle Joel said. "You may find yourself in a show of your own, with you as Fairy Godmother to a true-life Cinderella."

"Or not," Beth said.

"Or not," he echoed. "If it turns out badly, your mother can at least close that chapter in her life."

The couples separated as they reached the Montgomerys' car, and Brian drove Anwen home.

As he kissed her goodnight at her front door, he said, "These last few weeks with you have been very special to me. Not just searching the Internet together or going to a couple of movies, or even attending this terrific concert, but also our lunches in the park. Especially those." He kissed her once more, then backed away. "E-mail me from Wales," he said, waving.

"That's the plan!" Her face was illuminated by the porch light...and by the glow of her love for Brian. Yes, love. Yes, *glow*!

~   ~   ~

It was 5:00 a.m. in London, and David Lewellen had been awake for more than an hour. Nia had given him Susan's e-mail address the week before, but he hadn't yet summoned the courage to contact her. He wanted to—oh, yes, he wanted to; but he was nervous, anxious—oh, hell, he was terrified! He knew from her bio on the Web that she wasn't married, but what if she had a fiancé or a live-in lover? What if she didn't want to hear from him? What if she didn't answer his e-mail? Worse yet, what if she didn't remember him at all?

He turned on his bedside-table light so he could see the enlarged copy of their Great Orme snapshot in its silver frame. Most nights over the past twenty years he'd looked at it before falling asleep. Sometimes he even kissed it—just like a schoolboy—remembering their stolen moments on the Great Orme, and in Llandudno, and Trefriw, and anywhere they could steal them. God, how he'd loved her then...and since...and still.

Yes, he'd send her a message from the office on Monday. There was nothing to lose in trying. He couldn't possibly feel any more miserable than he did at this moment. He kissed the photo and put it away.

Good thing he'd had All England Tours to keep him busy all those years. Busy and happy. As happy as a man who'd lost his love could be. Yes, he'd e-mail Susan on Monday.

~   ~   ~

On Sunday evening, Susan and Annie left for Wales.

Part II
Allegro

Chapter 11

They had chosen a night flight so they could sleep on the plane and not waste time after arriving in Wales. The flight from Tallahassee to Atlanta was short, and the non-stop from Atlanta to Dublin, Ireland, was a comfortable eight-hour snooze. From there they boarded the ferry for a three-hour cruise to Holyhead on the northwest tip of Wales.

"I'm sorry we can't stop to see Dublin now," Susan said, as they settled into their seats on the huge ship. "That would have been fun."

"The goal, Mom. We have to stick to our goal."

"I know. But I'm scared. I'm trying not to think about Rhys."

Annie reached across the armrest and squeezed her mother's hand. "I guess if I were you I'd be a little scared too."

"What if we find him and he doesn't want to see me?"

"We can't go back to those 'what ifs.' They're endless. Besides, none of that matters. When we find him, he's either happy about it, or he's not. Or, face it, Mom, this adventure could have a bittersweet ending—he may still love you and not be able to act on it. A wife, children. Who knows? Whatever happens, you'll finally be able to stop wondering and worrying."

Susan sighed. "How did you get to be so knowledgeable at your age?"

"You taught me well."

"You're absolutely right—I did teach you well!" Susan elbowed her daughter and laughed. "And we're going to enjoy this...this vacation! Whatever happens!"

Both of them napped a little on the ship, and when they docked at Holyhead it was nine o'clock Monday morning, Wales time. They'd gained five hours since leaving Atlanta and the sun was shining. A sign at the ferry port, *Croeso i Cymru*, welcomed them to Wales.

They headed for the car rental station, wearing their backpacks and shoulder packs. The car ticketed to them was a Yaris, made by Toyota, and of course the steering wheel was on the right, the gearshift on the floor next to the driver. Annie was very glad that Susan wanted to drive. "I can't operate a shift car even when the handle is on the right, let alone the left!" she said. "Don't they believe in automatics over here?"

"This will be more fun."

"More fun than what?" Annie asked, though she was giggling.

They took the A55 to Bangor and continued with it along the northern coast, driving on what Annie called the wrong side of the road.

"Here in the U.K it's the right side," her mother said.

"No, it's the left side, and that's the wrong side." Annie was having a wonderful time, a big smile never leaving her face. She pointed out the green hills sprinkled with fat sheep, mountains in the distance, the clear waters of Conwy Bay, people riding bicycles, each time with the exclamation, "Look!"

Finally Susan laughed aloud. "You sound just like you did when you were three years old and your grandparents took us to Disney World. Every sentence started with 'Lookee, lookee!'"

"Can't help it, Mom. This is incredible! I am so glad you included me!"

"How could I not? You know all my secrets," she added with a smile. . . .*All but one*, she thought. *How can I tell her that Forrest Fletcher will soon be out of prison? The beast who fathered her, who promised he'd hunt me down. Yet I must tell her. Soon.*

None of the drive was familiar to Susan until they approached the old walled town of Conwy.

"Oh, my," Susan said, nearly breathless. "It hasn't changed a bit." The thick walls of stone and great towers loomed ahead.

"If Conwy has stayed the same for a few hundred years, then it wouldn't have changed in the last twenty," Annie said. "I think you're going to find all of your favorite spots in Wales just as you remember them."

They entered the town through a thick stone arch, one of three original "gateways," and Susan parked the car.

"What's the plan?" Annie asked.

"First, lunch. Then a visit to the Snowdonia Tours office."

~   ~   ~

London bustled with summer travelers, and All England Tours was reaping benefits—had been reaping benefits for years, growing into one of England's most respected and sought-after tour companies. Most of its business was generated at kiosks, strategically placed in tourist-arrival spots, particularly the one in downtown Victoria's Station, but David Lewellen preferred directing things from his quiet office suite on Norfolk Square, where his business had been located since the beginning. He never wanted to forget the beginning. Occasionally, he visited the outlying stations; Nia checked on them frequently.

"Time for lunch, Dad," Nia said, poking her head through the partially open door. "Jane and I are going around the block for some good Italian food at ASK before I head downtown. Want to join us?"

"Thanks, honey, but no. I've already ordered a sandwich from the deli."

Nia sighed and stepped into his office. "When are you going to eat a decent meal?"

"It's a veggie sandwich. That's decent."

"You know what I mean." She closed the door and moved toward his desk. "You've been existing on sandwiches and tins of beans since I gave you Susan's e-mail address. You can't get your mind off her, but you do nothing about it. You keep saying you're going to contact her, yet every time I ask, you say, 'I'll do it soon.'" She leaned over his desk. "So, did you send the message?"

David grinned at his daughter. "I'll do it soon," he said.

"You're impossible!"

"Actually, I'm going to send it this afternoon." He stood and came around the desk. "I promised myself over the weekend that this would be the day."

"Good! Now how about promising me?"

"That's a little harder to do…but, okay, I promise you." He kissed her forehead.

Nia started for the door, smiling. "If you order lunch from the deli tomorrow," she warned, pointing her finger at him, "I'll know you broke your promise."

The door closed behind her, and David returned to his desk, turning his chair to the window where he could look out over the Square with its colorful blooms and birds. What could he say to Susan? How could he possibly word the message so she wouldn't take offense? He didn't want to be flippant; he did not want to sound corny.…He just wanted her to know that he had never forgotten her, not for one minute.

~   ~   ~

They walked down Castle Street in Conwy toward Anna's Tea Room, Susan pointing first to one side of the street, then the other.

"That's Teapot World," she said. "Some of us girls went there with Mrs. Fleetwood. They have every kind of teapot you could imagine, and some you couldn't—like animal shapes and musical instruments. One pot even looked like a television set on legs!" She pointed toward the end of the block. "Down there is Aberconwy House, built in medieval times."

Annie was also enjoying the window displays in little shops showcasing Welsh crafts, particularly Celtic jewelry and beautiful sweaters made of soft wool. But there was no time to shop. They were on a mission.

"The castle, though," Annie said, imploring. "Can we take a little time to peek inside the castle before we leave Conwy? I've never even been *close* to a castle before today."

Susan slowed her steps. "Of course we can. Thank you for reminding me that this is our vacation, Annie. We'll *make* time for some fun!" She stopped at the next doorway. "And here is Anna's Tea Room. It's upstairs."

They had a lovely lunch at a window-table overlooking Castle Street, and finished with cups of steaming tea poured from a fat ceramic pot. "This is so nice, Mom," Annie said, as they left the tea room. "So nice to be with you."

"I like being with you, too. It's great to have you as a friend as well as my daughter. A nice change." Susan gave Annie a friendly pat on the shoulder.

The Snowdonia Tours office was on Rose Hill Street just off Lancaster Square, in an unimpressive little building, not at all what Susan had expected.

"I didn't visit the office back then," she said to Annie as they approached the door. "Rhys always came to us. I don't believe the Fleetwoods were here either."

They stepped into a spacious but cluttered reception area—travel books and leaflets everywhere, posters taking up every inch of wall space. A plate of Cadbury's chocolates rested on the counter with a small "Help Yourself" sign nestled close to it. The receptionist, who looked as if she hadn't yet been born when Rhys was an employee, was kind enough to get the bookkeeper, whom she said had "been around forever."

Mrs. Awbrey was a sweet lady who probably *had* been around forever, or nearly. She was a small, thin woman who looked to be in her mid-eighties.

"*Bore da*," Susan greeted her.

"Oh! *Ydych chi'n siarad Cymraeg?*"

Susan smiled. "No, I don't speak Welsh. Just a word or two."

"Well, you're a very nice girl. I can tell that already, I can."

Susan introduced Anwen and herself and said they would like to find Rhys Llewellyn.

Mrs. Awbrey's eyes lit up. "Please come back to my office, dears," she said, "where we can have a quiet little chat." It was obvious she was eager to talk. "Sit you down now," she said, offering two rather uncomfortable straight-backed chairs. "Would you like some tea?" She pointed to a pot snuggled into a cozy on her overloaded desk. "Nice cup o' tea, that. It's all ready."

Declining would not have been polite, so they accepted and waited patiently for Mrs. Awbrey to complete the pouring ritual.

Annie guessed, correctly, that the lady was a figurehead whose duties, one by one, had been overtaken by others as the years passed; she now had very little to do. As it turned out, Mrs. Awbrey was the owner's mother.

"My son started this business when he was fresh out of school," she said, proudly. "It's kept us both very nicely for many years. He never married, you see," she added in a whisper. "Now what was it you wanted to know? Oh, yes, about young Rhys Llewellyn. Well now, that was a tale, wasn't it?" She relaxed her frail body, settling more comfortably into her wing chair. "He was a fine young man, I tell you. A fine young man who was done wrong by that awful Mrs. Clougher. What did you say your connection to him is?"

"He, uh…I was part of a group he guided during the Llandudno Music and Arts Festival about twenty years ago," Susan said.

"Ah, yes. The *eisteddfod*. Now those festivals are really something, I can tell you. We have them all over Wales, look you, but the one in Llandudno has been going on for more than sixty years!"

"Yes, well, about Rhys Llewellyn—we became friends and corresponded for a while; then he disappeared."

Annie picked up the sentence. "So, while we're here on vacation, Mom thought it would be nice to find him, just for old times' sake, you know." She smiled and the lady was charmed.

"Ah, how nice! Then you don't know what happened?"

"We did learn about the accusation Mrs. Clougher made."

"Awful woman, just awful! Bossy, too. She was supposed to be the office manager and what did she do but steal from my son! Not only the money, but she was nicking small things, too—pencils and paper and the like. Lucky for us, we got the money back; well, not all of it, look you, but most."

Annie briefly wondered if Mrs. Awbrey had been the bookkeeper who didn't see the embezzlement until it was too late. Maybe that's why her duties had dwindled to little more than nothing. "We know that Mr. Llewellyn was exonerated," Annie said.

"*Diolch am hynny,* thank goodness for that!"

"But we never learned what happened to him afterward. Did he stay on here at Snowdonia Tours?" Susan already knew he had not, but she wanted to direct the conversation and keep Mrs. Awbrey on track.

"No, he didn't, and more's the pity. He felt we all had deserted him in his time of trouble, and I suspect we did, meself included, though we tried to make it up to him. My son offered him his job back, but young Rhys wouldn't take it. Didn't want to work with those of us who'd turned our backs on him. Can't say as I blame him."

"So where did he go? Did he continue to work in the tour business somewhere else?"

"Now let me think… I believe I heard that he set up a little tour company of his own somewhere south of here, but I'm not sure where, or what it was called. Maybe in Llanrwst or Betws-y-Coed. There are plenty of tourists down that way because of Snowdonia Valley, you know, and the mountains. There's a narrow-gauge train that takes people on a delightful sight-seeing ride across the mountains from Blaenau Ffestiniog over to Porthmadog. You girls should ride that train and see our lovely mountains," she said, gesturing with her hands. She stopped suddenly, hands in mid-air. "Hmm. Maybe that's where young Rhys went, Blaenau Ffestiniog. Wouldn't surprise me."

"Would your son have more information?" Susan asked.

"No, dear." She put her hands against her chest. "He was embarrassed by the whole thing and determined to put it behind him. Bad for business, you know. I remember shortly after Rhys left, I wanted to send him a note of encouragement, but my son asked me not to. He said he didn't know where the boy went and he didn't want to know. 'Just let it be, Mother,' he said. 'Just let it be.' …So I did." She sighed, and folded her hands in her lap.

Back outside, Susan and Annie faced Lancaster Square.

"Well, that was useless," Annie said.

"Not entirely. We'll check out those little towns she mentioned. Surely, somebody will know something about Rhys."

Annie turned her attention to the column in the center of the Square. "Yet another spelling of Llewellyn," she said, reading the marker honoring Llywelyn the Great, the town's founder.

"Llewellyn in Wales is like Smith and Jones in the United States."

"Hmmm. I wonder if Rhys is a descendant of the Great Llywelyn himself."

Susan laughed. "I'm sure all Llewellyns would claim to be. This one was the first official Prince of Wales and the country's last independent ruler."

"How do you know that?"

"I've been reading up on Llewellyns," Susan said, dryly.

Annie gave her a thumbs-up. "So where do we go from here?"

"To Llandudno—you made our reservations at the Clarence, remember. And thank you for that, Annie. It will be just like old times for me! We'll spend the night there, then head south, as Mrs. Awbrey indicated—Bodnant Garden, Trefriw, Betws-y-Coed, Blaenau Ffestiniog—wherever the trail takes us. But first…" She turned and faced her daughter. "To the castle!"

~   ~   ~

At the same time that Susan and Annie ascended the walkway to Conwy Castle, David Lewellen sat in his London office, once again reading the e-mail message he had composed hours before. Finally, more or less satisfied with the wording, he pushed "Send."

~   ~   ~

Back in the United States, as David's e-mail message made its way through cyberspace, Forrest Fletcher stepped out of prison and into the sunshine, a free man for the first time in nineteen years.

Chapter 12

Forrest Fletcher rode a Greyhound bus to Davenport, Georgia. He still owned the 1200-acre farm five miles out of town, where it was "safe" for him to live. Or, rather, where children would be safe from him—*what a load of shit*, he thought. As a registered sex offender, he was prohibited from living or working within a thousand feet of places where minors congregate—*yeah, yeah*—*if the stupid law doesn't get repealed when stupid people realize that registered sex offenders can't live anywhere! Kids are everywhere, all over the place.* Well, Fletcher had enough acreage that it didn't matter one damn to him, law or no law.

His father's prosperous farm—the farm where Fletch had started his own crop-dusting business all those years ago—was waiting for his return, though his father was no longer there. Pops had died the year before without ever once visiting his son in prison. *The son of a bitch. Shut me out of his life like I was some kind of monster and he was a saint. Some saint. He didn't mind taking over my business after I was gone, selling my planes, adding another million to his fortune. Lucky I signed it over to him, with conditions of course. Well, guess what, Pops? The money's all mine now, and I'm going to spend it like I damn please!*

Fletch walked down the driveway toward the house he'd lived in for more than half his life. It was deserted but far from run down. Just like him. He'd been deserted by his only living relative and all those self-righteous Davenport citizens he'd sucked up to years before. But, like his house, he was far from run down. He wasn't a kid any more. He was forty-nine years old, smarter, and stronger. Yes, he had plenty of good years left and plenty of money to enjoy them. To settle some old scores.

He looked toward the back of the property, at the empty hangars, empty except for one lonely crop-duster, his favorite; he could see it from where he stood. Couldn't figure out why Pops kept that one when he sold the others.

Maybe he had a soft spot in his heart for me after all. Fletch was glad the plane was there. *I'll start it up one of these days,* he thought, *and fly it like I used to. Have some fun. Stir up dust, rather than dispense it.* He laughed at the image.

An off-site caretaker had been maintaining the property, paid through a trust Pops had set up when he knew he was dying. Fletch would keep the caretaker on. Why should he do manual labor? Did enough of that in prison. *Shit, what a life! For a while I had everything—great business, some back-slapping buddies, townspeople who thought I was really somebody. Even Pops was proud of me.* Fletch clenched his fists and his jaw, feeling more angry with every step. It wasn't his fault he'd lost it all—it was hers! *No one needed to know about my little hobby; no one ever would have known if that bitch hadn't turned me in. I never thought she would, Miss Fancy Musician with a fancy career ahead of her. I thought she'd be too embarrassed and ashamed, like the others. . . . Okay, Susan Damn Evans, you ruined my life—now I'll ruin yours!*

There was a time when Forrest Fletcher had wanted to be a musician. He could really sing. He'd had a guitar and played it damn well too. Until that stupid contest. Maybe if his mother had stuck around instead of running off when he was a kid, he wouldn't have taken it so hard. Losing that contest to a thirteen-year-old brat had made him so mad that he went home and smashed his guitar over a fence post. He'd find some other way to make Pops proud.

Fletch had loved crop-dusting, loved being an agricultural daredevil. Besides providing a needed service (which was important to his position among the town fathers) and earning good money (not only important but crucial), the profession afforded him a "high"—he loved the pun—like no other. It was incredible—the fast climbs, sharp mid-air turns, and swooping close to the ground across a soybean, peanut, or tobacco field, dispensing pesticides and herbicides. Sometimes he landed on a road or in a field next to a store where he could get a beer, just for the hell of it. But times had changed during his prison term. The law no longer tolerated barnstorming antics, and the need for crop-dusters had diminished. Fletch knew that many crop-duster pilots were now using their talents to help clean up oil spills, eradicate cocaine- and heroine-producing plants, or fight forest fires. *What a bunch of goody-goody crap,* he thought.

He'd learned a lot in prison. He'd learned it didn't pay to be soft. And he'd learned that even the tough guys, the hardened criminals, had no time for sex offenders. They'd beat him up a couple of times when the guards weren't looking, calling him a pervert and worse. Imagine! A pervert, for doing what comes naturally! Susan Evans had no idea what she'd put him through, sending him to prison—the torture of living like a real criminal, day in, day out, year after year. Okay, so his life as an upstanding citizen had been a sham. But it was a good sham while it lasted. He'd had it all. And all it had cost him was some glad-handing, phony smiles crap. He'd only served on the city council and on the church board to give himself a social boost anyway. Well, there'd be no more pretending for him. He was tough now, his own man. Didn't need people any more; didn't want them. And didn't need or want crop-dusting either. *There's no fun in it any more. And where there's no fun, there's no Fletch.*

It didn't matter to Forrest Fletcher that the crop-dusting industry had dried up. Before prison, he'd begun building a nice little nest egg, and his father had increased it many times over, playing with farm futures, day-trading, buying and selling stocks of stuff he never saw. He'd been doing that since before Fletch was born. First it was the telephone, then some kind of ticker-tape machine that spewed paper all over the floor. Got rich just sitting on his ass. *Too bad you couldn't take it with you, Pops. I'll do just fine with it.*

He stepped through the front door of his large farmhouse and looked around. It had been built in 1915 and well kept over the years. Looked a little different now, though. Obviously, his father had done some renovating before he died. The original hardwood floors were still intact but now shone with new finish. Crystal chandeliers hung from high ceilings in the living and dining rooms. Curtains throughout the house were new, as were the oriental rugs. The kitchen was modern, with one o' them "island" things in the middle; looked nothing like the old kitchen Fletch remembered. He sighed. He liked it. The only thing missing was a damn computer. He'd have to get one. He'd learned about computers in prison. Knew how to use one, to surf the Net, to send e-mail, and to do some illegal stuff too. He'd have a great time playing with Susan Evans. Before he *really* played with her, that is. Now *that* would be fun!

~   ~   ~

Susan and Anwen checked into the Clarence Hotel on Gloddaeth Street in Llandudno then walked through the town. Trying to drive a car, much less find places to park, would have been pointless, since so many people had gathered for the festival. They had come from every corner of the globe—dancers, folksingers, instrumentalists, artists and craftspeople. There were concert tents and other busy venues, many that Susan remembered from so long ago—St. Johns and Holy Trinity churches, the Dunoon Hotel just a block from the Clarence, the Bandstand on the North Shore Promenade. Her eyes were wide with excitement.

"Annie, so much is the same! Just like twenty-five years ago—I feel like a schoolgirl on a field trip once again! This is such fun!"

"Is there any place here we can ask about Rhys?"

"Hmmm. Probably not. The festival personnel will have changed, and Rhys wasn't actually involved with music and art, other than as our guide. He wasn't a musician, but he did love music, Annie. It was through him that I first heard a Welsh harp. So beautiful." She sighed. "I think our best chance at finding Rhys lies south of here, in the little towns Mrs. Awbrey mentioned. She said he started his own business. Even if it's not operating any more—and we couldn't find any evidence of it on the Internet—surely someone will remember."

They left the Promenade and circled back past Oriel Mostyn, the gallery where Susan's old school friend, Scott Williams, and others had exhibited some of their artwork in a special room. Without realizing it, Susan reached for her locket, rubbing it between her fingers. It was Scott's work under the clasp—the photo he had snapped at the Great Orme and Susan had cut apart so that her face and Rhys's would fit into each side, touching each other.

"Having a good memory, Mom?" Anwen asked.

Susan smiled. "Mmmhmm." Susan reminded her daughter of the picture she had shown her a few weeks before, when Annie had asked about the locket. And she told her about Scott, the boy who had snapped the picture and had displayed some of his artwork in this very gallery. With that, her mind traveled to the Great Orme and her love for Rhys, the handsome young man she still loved with all her heart.

"I'm getting tired," she said. "After all night on the plane and ferry, the drive to Conwy and then here, I'm more than tired—I'm exhausted! Let's find something to eat, then go back to the hotel and call it a day."

They stopped at a cozy pub on Lloyd Street, where they settled in front of an enormous fireplace and enjoyed bowls of cawl, a traditional Welsh soup, steaming hot and brimming with potatoes, cabbage, leeks, bacon and lamb. It was delicious, and Susan was tempted to chase it down with some Welsh whiskey, as other diners were doing. But she declined in favor of the ever-present teapot.

Annie drank the whiskey.

~ ~ ~

Early the next morning—Tuesday—as they checked out of the hotel, Anwen spoke to the desk clerk, an older gentleman. "Would you be acquainted with tour companies in the area, the ones that guide groups to the festival?"

"Well, yes, ma'am. Snowdonia Tours out of Conwy usually runs a van or two."

"Any others? I'm thinking particularly of one that might have come here about fifteen years ago from farther south in the valley."

"Ah, no. I've only come here last year meself. From Cardiff, y'see. Wanted to escape the city when I retired, take a less stressful job in me sunset years."

Though she smiled, Anwen's face registered disappointment.

"Our porter, Mr. Cretney, now," the man offered, "he's been here more'n thirty years. Shall I ring him for you?"

"Oh, would you? Please!"

At that, Susan quickly took interest. "Annie, you're a wonder! I didn't think to ask about older hotel staff."

Annie thanked the clerk and they seated themselves on an overstuffed sofa in the lobby. All around them, folks were chatting in a mixture of English and Welsh. The wait was short. And Mr. Cretney wasn't nearly as old as they'd imagined, probably in his early fifties and in excellent physical condition. "Good morning, ladies!" he said. "What may I do for you?"

"Please sit down, Mr. Cretney," Susan said with a smile. She introduced herself and her daughter. "We're hoping you can help us locate someone who was a frequent visitor to Llandudno many years ago. I understand you've been with the Clarence Hotel for a long time."

"Aye, that I have. Started working here right after my eighteenth birthday back in 1973. Never saw a need to go anywhere else." He sat opposite them and leaned forward, elbows on his knees. He had a friendly face and an easy demeanor, and Susan liked him at once.

"Well...uh." Susan had a hard time getting started. She cleared her throat and began again. "I was here in 1987, at the Clarence Hotel, I mean. I was a musician—well, I still am, classical guitar—and I came to the *eisteddfod* with a group from my school. We had a guide from Snowdonia Tours, who showed us some of your lovely country and stayed with us throughout the festival, attended our concerts, and...well, became our friend. We stayed in touch by mail for almost a year, but then he stopped writing and...uh, none of our group ever heard from him again. I hope you can help. It would be wonderful to see him once more, if for no other reason than to thank him for a vacation I'll never forget."

"And what was this gentleman's name?"

Susan swallowed. "Rhys. Rhys Llewellyn."

Mr. Cretney sat back in his chair. His strong shoulders slumped, and he stared into space. "Ah, young Rhys," he said, finally. "I think of him as young Rhys because I never saw him grow old. I first knew him when he came to Arnhall Orphanage, where I myself had lived since being dumped on the doorstep at birth." Mr. Cretney's breath came out in a long sigh. "Rhys was a feisty little four-year-old and I was sixteen. I was assigned to him as a sort of big brother." He looked at Susan and at once recognized the hope in her eyes. He spoke kindly. "I can't tell you where he is, young lady, since I don't know. And I don't know anyone else who knows either. But I can tell you where he *was*, if that would help."

"Oh, yes, please!" Susan was now on the edge of her seat, and Anwen was clutching the sofa's armrest.

"I can tell by your face that you already know about the trouble he was in, no fault of his own." Susan nodded, and Mr. Cretney continued. "Well, when he left here, he moved to Betws-y-Coed and became a freelance tour guide. We were still in touch then; he often consulted me, as his big brother. He bought a small passenger van and painted 'Tour Wales' on the side. Started taking tourists about, mostly to the Blaenau Ffestiniog area. He loved riding that little train to Porthmadog." Mr. Cretney chuckled at the memory. "Even took me with him once."

"So, did 'Tour Wales' become the company he'd always dreamed of owning?" Susan asked.

"Ah, no. He was only in Betws-y-Coed for about a year, then up and left. ... I never heard from him again."

Susan's disappointment was obvious.

"We can go to Betws-y-Coed, Mom," Anwen suggested. "And ask around. Maybe someone there can help."

Mr. Cretney cleared his throat. "Ladies, I...uh, I have to tell you that young Rhys...well...he got married."

Susan reached for her locket, and Annie reached for her mother's other hand.

Chapter 13

"He married Brisen Devenallt, another Arnhall orphan. She was a nice girl," Mr. Cretney added, almost reluctantly. He watched the tears form in Susan's eyes, then leaned forward once again, speaking softly. "You said your name is Susan Evans. . . . You're *his* Susan, aren't you?"

Susan blinked, and the unshed tears fell. She could not speak.

Mr. Cretney nodded. "I thought so. All these years later, and you still look just as he described you, just like your picture. That boy, my 'little brother,' was so much in love with you, he could talk to me of little else."

Anwen handed her mother a tissue. "Mom still keeps his photo in her locket," she said, indicating. "May I?" she asked her mother, reaching for the clasp. Susan nodded and Anwen removed the locket, handing it to Mr. Cretney.

He opened it and looked inside. "This is the picture I meant. Young Rhys had one just like it—his was all of a piece, though. Said it was taken at the Great Orme. Very proud of it, he was. Proud of you, too, Susan." Susan buried her face in the tissue and wept.

The nice gentleman joined her on the sofa and put his arm around her. "I don't know why Rhys married Brisen," he said. "That was one thing he would never discuss with me, and I couldn't figure it out. She also lived at the orphanage and was like a dear sister to him. I knew he didn't love her the way he loved you. When he told me he'd married Brisen, I couldn't help asking about you. He said to me, 'I will always love Susan.' . . . Just like that. And there was to be no more discussion of his personal life." He sighed. "After that, we drifted apart, the way folks do over time. I heard he left Betws-y-Coed during that next year. . . . Brisen's gone too."

He handed the locket across to Anwen, who fastened it back onto her mother's neck. "I'm sorry if I made you sad, Susan," he said, "but I felt I should tell you. I owe it to you, and to Rhys. After all, you made this trip especially to find him, didn't you? The truth now."

Susan wiped her eyes and managed a smile. "You found me out, Mr. Cretney." She took his hand in hers. "Thank you. . . . Thank you very much."

"What will you do now?"

Susan straightened her shoulders, her voice once again strong. "We're going to Betws-y-Coed," she said. "I can't stop looking now. I just want to see him one more time, to know that he's happy. . . . I need closure."

They stood, and he walked them to the front door, ever the gentleman. He called the valet for them and helped put their luggage into the car. And as they drove away, he remained in sight. And stayed there for several minutes after the car was gone, thinking, remembering. . . . He hoped he had done the right thing.

~   ~   ~

The late-morning sun that had shone so beautifully the day before was in hiding as Susan and Anwen drove south on the A470. The air was misty, a "soft" day in Wales, but the weather did nothing to further dampen the spirits of the women in the car—Susan's spirits were already dampened somewhat by the news that Rhys was married, but she remained focused on her mission with a pleasant determination that her daughter found admirable.

Annie was a bit more upbeat but she, too, was cautious. "How far it is to Betws-y-Coed?" she asked.

"Not far. Less than twenty miles," Susan answered. "But we have two stops to make before we get there, and the first is just seven miles away. I want to visit the café at Bodnant Garden. Actually, it's called a tea room. It's where Rhys had arranged for us to hear an Irish harp. It was the first time I had ever heard one, and I was completely swept away. I just want to see the place, to do a little remembering."

"Sounds good to me."

"A cup of tea and some scones might be nice, too," Susan said, smiling.

"That sounds even better, but I'd prefer a good cup of coffee."

"You might find a cup of coffee in Wales, but I can't promise it will be good!"

"Hmmph. What's the second stop?"

"Trefriw, the little village where Catrin Fenna's grandparents lived. Our group gave a concert there on our second night in Wales. . . . Trefriw is where I fell in love with Rhys." Susan's mind wandered to their stolen moments that night, their walk beneath the trees, their first kiss and the way it made her skin prickle all over. She was so lost in the past that she nearly missed the turn into the Garden.

"There, Mom! There's the sign!" Annie said, pulling her back to the present.

Susan turned into the shady car park, where a handful of other visitors were already walking toward the café. Mist still clung stubbornly to the air but the scent was fresh and clean. As they ascended the wooden steps, Susan again felt as if she were stepping back in time. Inside, the tea room looked essentially the same, the tables perhaps arranged a bit differently, but there was no harpist on this day.

"There," Susan whispered to Annie, as she pointed to the right. "Right there against that wall, that's where the harpist was. He was playing as we came in. People were eating quietly and listening; no one was talking."

Anwen gazed around the pretty room, a little surprised to find it smaller than she had imagined from her mother's description. Plenty of tables, but with a cozy atmosphere. They approached the counter, picked up trays and ordered tea and scones. At the end near the cashier was a basket of CDs for sale.

"Oh, look Annie!" Susan said, quickly picking up a CD. "Harp music!" She scanned the selections on the back of the case. "Some of the same songs I heard all those years ago. I have to have one of these!"

"Our harpist is quite famous," said the cashier, a touch of pride in her voice. "I'm sorry he's not here today to play for you."

"Me too," Susan said, smiling. She paid for her treasure and their food, and they sat at one of the wooden tables to enjoy a few minutes rest.

Annie scanned the back of the CD case as she sipped her tea. "'Summertime.' 'The Rose.' I know those songs."

Susan smiled to herself, remembering the time she played and sang "The Rose" for Rhys—their private concert in the little anteroom at the church in Trefriw.

"Oh, here's a song called 'Rhys.'"

"Let me see." Susan took the case. "'Rhys.' I heard that one on the day my group was here! Very pretty, kind of reverent-sounding. I remember asking Rhys about it—he told me the title, then laughed and said it was a Welsh hymn, nothing to do with himself!"

When they finished their tea and scones, they went outside and walked a short distance up one of the paths. They were just in time to see the mist rise and the sun appear over the top of Bodnant House in the distance. A beautiful sight.

"Guess we'll have good weather for the rest of our drive," Annie remarked.

"Or for the next few hours. Or few minutes," Susan said. "In Wales, one never knows." She sighed, remembering her walk in Bodnant Garden with Rhys. The sun had been shining that day, in more ways than one. The Laburnum Arch was radiant with golden flowers, and Susan had felt the radiance as if it were emanating from her own skin. Maybe it was. Rhys's arm had brushed against hers as they walked. Angie and Scott were walking ahead... "Ahhhh..." Her sigh was audible.

~   ~   ~

A slight detour took them across the river to the B5106, a winding, hilly road leading into Trefriw. It was a pretty drive, with clumps of gorse and bracken sprinkled alongside. The road was narrow, however, and made their small rental car seem enormous.

Annie was apprehensive. "I'm glad there are no cars coming the other way! This is hard on my nerves!"

"We're barely crawling, Annie."

"Good. Let's keep it that way." He eyes were glued to the road ahead.

Just then a little sports car came into view over the top of the hill and zipped past them on the right. Annie ducked, as if that would do any good.

Susan laughed. "Did he scare you a little?"

"A lot! How much further?"

They crested the hill. "There 'tis," Susan said. Trefriw lay before them.

"Looks like it might fall off the mountain any minute."

"Not a chance. Been here for hundreds of years."

Susan parked the car and they began walking along the main street. A sign was anchored to the rock wall, which lined the sidewalk, and Annie stopped to read. "Look," she said. "They actually post distances in miles, as well as kilometers. Betws-y-Coed is five miles from here. But look at these other places—I still don't see how they can pronounce this stuff—Gwydyr, Llanrhychwyn! Oh, by the way, Brian's Welsh accent is adorable, don't you agree? And I love the way he says my name!"

Susan rolled her eyes. "Something tells me you love everything about Brian."

She may have been kidding, but Annie was serious. "Mom, I think I'm falling in love with Brian," she said.

"You *think*?"

"Okay, I am in love with him."

Susan looked intently at her eighteen-year-old daughter.

"What?" Annie said. "Am I too young to be in love?"

"Annie, think about where we are right now and why we're here. How can you ask me such a question? I was in love at sixteen and I knew it was real. I still know it." Her tone softened. "Of course you're not too young to be in love. What you do with that love, how you treat it, whether you make responsible choices regarding it—those are the things to consider. If you're asking me if you should quit college before you even start, and get married, my reply would have to be No. You and Brian are both intelligent people with exciting lives ahead of you. If you plan together, and dream together…and prepare yourselves—individually—to *be* together, you'll have it all."

Annie's smile was shy. "Thanks, Mom."

They climbed the steep hill, past rows of stone cottages, to the church where Susan had played in recital so many years before; then they turned to look out over the paved path they had walked, and on across the valley to the rolling hills beyond the river. Annie kept quiet, allowing her mother time with her memories.

When they arrived back down at the main street, Susan pointed to a building on the corner. "Let's go in here," she said.

"Bwyty Glanrafon," Annie read, garbling the sounds. "What's that?"

"A café."

"A café? We just ate!"

"We had tea and scones. It's lunchtime now."

"Are you honestly hungry?"

"Doesn't matter. A café, any café, is a great place to get information."

Books and magazines—in addition to food—were for sale inside, and Susan perused them while their sandwiches were being prepared. Annie, who was more thirsty than hungry, sat at a table and gulped a bottle of lemonade.

A tiny voice stopped her in mid-gulp. "You shouldn't drink so fast!"

Surprised, Annie looked down at a pretty little girl, about three years old, who stood beside her. "Oh, I'm sorry," she said, smiling at the child. "Please forgive my bad manners. I hope you don't drink fast."

"No! Me mum would never allow it."

Just then the child's mother spoke to her from the next table. "Brisen! You mustn't bother the nice lady. Come here at once."

"No!" Annie said quickly. "She's no bother at all. She's very polite and very pretty too." The child lowered her head and smiled. "What is your name?" Annie asked her. She was sure she had heard correctly, but wanted to confirm.

"Brisen," the child replied, shyly.

"What a beautiful name! I've never known anyone called Brisen."

"Me neither."

Annie spoke to the child's mother, who looked to be only a few years older than Annie herself. "Is Brisen a popular name in Wales?"

The mother smiled. "No, not really. When I was about her age, I wandered away from home, and a nice young woman named Brisen found me and took care of me until she could locate my mother. I had been too upset at getting lost to tell her who I was, so it took some doing. She, of course, called the constable for help, but she wouldn't leave my side even when he took over. She sang to me and gave me a cookie, and assured me that she would return me to my mother. And she did. And every couple of weeks she'd check up on me, to see if I was still fine and all." The woman smiled at the memory. "I never forgot her; so, when my little girl was born, I named her Brisen after that nice lady. Very pretty, she was. Me da said she was a 'smashing looker,' was Brisen Devenallt!" The woman laughed.

By then, Susan had joined Annie at the table and had heard most of the story. She was too stunned to speak, so Annie spoke for her. "This lady, Brisen, does she live in Trefriw?"

"Oh no. Never did, that I know of. She worked at the woolen mill just down the street, but she lived in Betws-y-Coed, a short drive from here. That's what made it all the more remarkable that she stayed with me that day, not one bit anxious to get on home."

"Well, maybe she didn't have a family of her own and had no reason to hurry home," Susan injected, fishing.

"Oh, she did marry sometime after that, but I didn't know his name. She quit her job soon after she married, and we—me mum and me—never heard from her again. Well, we did hear that she had a baby. I was glad, too. She would've been a wonderful mother."

~   ~   ~

David Lewellen checked his e-mail for the umpteenth time. Still no reply from Susan.

Chapter 14

"A baby. ….She had a baby." They were standing on the porch of the cafe, and Susan's eyes filled with tears. "Rhys is a father," she whispered.

Annie's voice was gentle. "And you're a mother. Wouldn't you expect that, after all this time?"

"His child would be about your age now." Susan gripped the railing, closed her eyes and mentally calculated the years, based on what she had learned from Mr. Cretney and the young woman at the café. "The child would be older than you, almost a whole year." She turned to look at Anwen. "Rhys didn't wait for me. And before you say anything—I had no choice! Remember?" Her eyes squeezed shut. "Oh, Annie, I'm sorry. I didn't mean…"

"I know you didn't. I know you love me." Annie's hand was on her mother's shoulder. "But maybe there were extenuating circumstances for Rhys, too. Mr. Cretney said that he couldn't figure out why Rhys married Brisen, that she was like a dear sister to him."

"Well, it's obvious *why* he married her. He got her pregnant."

"Or someone else did."

The silence was nearly palpable. Finally, Susan released her grip on the rail. "You're right, Annie," she said. "It's not fair of me to judge. I know nothing about his circumstances."

"And that's why we're here. Because you want to know. You want closure, you said it yourself. C'mon. Let's visit the mill where she worked."

As the young woman had said, the woolen mill was "just down the street," but they found no one there who remembered Brisen Devenallt from twenty years ago. "Ah, the mill workers, they come and go, and twenty years is a long time past," they were told. They were offered a tour of the mill but declined.

"Are ye sure now?" a kind gentleman with an elf-like face asked. "We've got it all—warping, weaving, hanking, carding, spinning and spanking!"

He was cute and funny, and it was hard to turn him down, but neither Susan nor Anwen was in the mood for a tour.

Susan had a sudden thought. She asked the gentleman, "Do you know Mr. Siam Whittal? I believe he lives here in Trefriw." Why hadn't she remembered the name before? Rhys had said in one of his letters that Mr. Whittal was going to match the money Rhys had saved to get started in business.

"*Lived*, dear lady. Lived. Mr. Whittal passed on some years ago. An orphan he was, and an orphan he died—no family, y'see. Left a big lot o' money to the church, he did. Mr. Whittal was a great man. So, ladies, if ye won't take the tour, won'tcha stop in our mill store and look around a bit?"

That caught Anwen's attention. They thanked him and entered the store. Inside were beautiful sweaters, scarves, caps and other woven items. "Just remember," her mother warned, "whatever you buy has to fit into your backpack, and that's pretty full already." ·

"I saved more room in mine than you did in yours," Annie said, grinning. "I planned for this kind of, uh, emergency. This scarf will fit in just fine." The one she snatched up and carried to the register was a soft mauve. "Perfect with my deep purple jacket!"

Fifteen minutes later they arrived in Betws-y-Coed. "Shall we look for a hotel?" Anwen asked.

"What I'd really like to find is a nice bed-and-breakfast place, quiet, out of the way, comfy. There's a post office over there. Let's stop and ask."

"Maybe we could find out about Rhys at the same time," Annie said.

"I doubt if they'd say, though you never know when someone might want to chat. Folks in this country do love to talk."

"Yeah. A weird mixture of Welsh and English," Annie said. "I'm never quite sure what I'm hearing."

"Let's try." Susan opened the post office door and they stepped inside. There was a line and, sure enough, plenty of incomprehensible chatter.

When it was their turn, they asked about a guest house. "The bookshop on the next street has a rack of free pamphlets describing all sorts of nice places to stay. That's the place to look, *or gore*, all right," the postal clerk said, firmly. She was short and a bit chubby, and her smile—if she ever had one—was nonexistent on this day. Too, the long line of customers had grown behind Susan and Annie. They thanked her and left.

"Well, that one wasn't much of a talker. What was that last thing she said?" Annie asked.

"Who knows? She's tired and busy, and probably feels cranky. I was actually *afraid* to ask her about Rhys," Susan added, laughing. "Let's hit the bookshop."

The rack inside the door held brochures of all kinds—accommodations, restaurants, attractions and activities. The store wasn't particularly busy, and two of the workers were standing around with helpful—hopeful?—looks on their faces. Susan approached them, holding out one of the pamphlets.

"Can you recommend a nice bed-and-breakfast place, not too far from town? We'd like to stay a night or two."

"Oh, certainly I can," the pretty blond girl answered. "There are several along the A5, both ends of the village." She leafed through the pamphlet. "Look here. This one's very nice. It's an old rectory, restored. I've heard their breakfast is to die for—baked beans, tomatoes, fry-ups and such. And here. Oh!" She tapped her polished fingernail on a picture of a cozy-looking cottage with a slate roof. "Me mother's cousins stayed here just last winter. They said the inside was all decorated in shades of peach and green, real pretty. If you're looking for something quiet, this is the one I'd recommend. It has a lake alongside and a walking path."

Susan thanked her and said they would call to see if a room was available. "I have another question," she said, knowing the girls were much too young but hoping they could provide a lead. "Did you ever hear of a tour-guide company called Tour Wales?"

Both girls burst out laughing, and the brunette answered. "I do believe every touring van around here is labeled Tour Wales or some variation of it!"

"I understand. The one I'm looking for was probably in service here before you were born anyway."

"Oh, in that case, ask the lady at the B&B." She pointed again to the one with the peachy-green décor, the one that Susan had decided to call. "The lady, Miss Jervis, and her mum, Mrs. Jervis—who's really old—have lived in that house for many, many years."

"That settles it then. We'll make a reservation. Is there a public phone nearby?"

Fortunately, a room was available for that night and the next, and Susan and Anwen drove straight there to check in. Their upstairs room had two twin beds and was *en suite*, meaning it had its own bathroom, an important consideration since many B&Bs offered only rooms with a shared bath.

Annie flopped onto one of the beds. "Let's stay here for a couple of hours," she said. "We've got plenty of time to do the town."

Susan laughed. "We're not exactly going to 'do the town.' We're going to have dinner and ask questions."

"We're going to get nosy. My kind of entertainment!"

Susan pulled off her shoes and stretched out on the other bed. Before long, they both were napping.

~ ~ ~

It was late morning in Davenport, Georgia, hot and humid. Gnats were buzzing Forrest Fletcher's ears, sticking, making him itch as he walked around his property. Sometimes he blew at them out of the sides of his mouth, but he really didn't mind. He liked gnats, with their fearless buzz and bite. They reminded him of his crop-dusters. He'd been thinking a lot about Susan Evans lately, about how she'd ruined his life, his perfect life. He was going to buzz and bite her, just like a pesky gnat. E-mail messages. That's the way he'd start. He'd ordered a computer over the phone. Didn't want to go into town where all those fingers would point at him. It was bad enough going to the country store for supplies, hoping he didn't run into anyone who knew him. Fortunately, the clerks at that store didn't know his name and couldn't know him by sight; his appearance had changed a lot over the last nineteen wasted damn years. He was scrawnier, had started growing a scruffy little beard, and had plans for a ponytail—even a tiny short one—as soon as his hair was long enough to get hold of. Didn't have to primp any more for those hotsy-totsy townspeople. Computer should arrive tomorrow by courier. Then he'd begin his campaign of terror. He wouldn't reveal his name, and he'd hide behind an untraceable address—his cellmate had been a sneaky geek bastard who'd taught him well. Damn! He was getting hot and hard just thinking about how scared Susan Evans would be!

~ ~ ~

David Lewellen had had an extremely busy morning; so busy in fact, that it was mid-afternoon before he remembered lunch. Just as he reached for the phone to order a sandwich, his daughter tapped on the door and stepped inside.

She scowled at him. "Are you ordering lunch from the deli?"

"Uh..." He quickly recalled what she'd said the day before, that if he ordered a meager lunch from the deli, she would know he had not sent Susan a message. "I, uh, was about to ring your favorite restaurant and have a real Italian meal sent over."

Nia laughed. "Sure you were! Don't let me stop you."

He put the phone down. "I'll do it in a minute. And, yes, I did send the message. Yesterday."

"And?"

"And nothing. ...Not one word."

"It's early yet. Maybe she doesn't check her messages every day, or every night. Some people only check e-mail on weekends."

David groaned. "Oh, this is torture. Why did I let you talk me into it?"

"Hey there! Don't blame me." She perched on the side of his desk. "You wanted to all along. I was just the enabler. ...You'll hear from her, Dad," she added softly. "I know you will."

"I wish I were as sure as you are. I'm nervous, just like a kid." He looked at his daughter and smiled. "You're a good girl, Nia. I love you a whole bunch."

She laughed. "That's what you used to say when I was a child—I love you a whole bunch."

"It's still true. It always will be. So, have you had lunch?"

"Of course. Hours ago. I wouldn't mind a cup of tea, though, if you'd take me somewhere. I could sit with you and watch you eat. A *real* meal."

He stood, shrugging his shoulders in mock surrender. "Let's go!"

~   ~   ~

A light tapping on the bedroom door woke Susan from her nap. Annie slept on, blissfully unaware.

"Miz Evans?" The voice was that of the elder Jervis woman. Susan jumped up and opened the door.

"Yes, Mrs. Jervis?"

"I have a—" She stopped, seeing the slumbering Annie on the bed nearest the window. "Oh, dear, I've disturbed you! I'm so very sorry!"

"Not at all, Mrs. Jervis. Please come in. It's time we moved around a bit anyway."

Annie started to stir, then sat up, rubbing her eyes.

"I just wanted you to know," the lady said, "that I have a lovely tea ready for you in the dining room whenever you'd like to have it."

Susan looked at her watch. It was four o'clock. "I think right now would be perfect! Would you join us?"

"Oh, no. I couldn't," she said, but her eyes brightened. She was probably in her eighties; a slight hump pushed her shoulders up in back; her skin was like parchment. Susan guessed the lady was lonely and enjoyed having company.

"Please?" Susan begged politely.

"Well, maybe for just one cup." Mrs. Jervis smiled shyly. "I'll see you downstairs."

As Susan shut the door, Annie whispered, "We've done nothing but eat since we arrived in Wales!"

"And we're going to eat some more. Remember, this is the lady who's been living here since time began. She may know something about Rhys."

"I'll go home looking like a toad!"

Chapter 15

The tea was simple, Mrs. Jervis explained, rather than elaborate because, she said, "I know you Americans like your dinner, and I don't want to fill you up beforehand; just a lovely tea to hold you over. Would you like me to pour?"

"Please," Susan answered. The china teacups were so delicate that Susan was afraid to let her teeth touch them, lest they chip!

That didn't worry Annie, but the food did—not its presentation, rather the amount of it. *This is a* simple *tea?* she wondered. She wasn't hungry. How could she politely decline? . . . She could not.

"Please have some *bara brith*," Mrs. Jervis said, indicating a speckled-looking bread, "and some of this too. It's called *teisen mel.*" She held a plate toward Annie. "It's a honey cake." Annie smiled but hesitated. "Or perhaps you would prefer a scone," the lady suggested. "I made them myself. They're filled with currants, they are."

Susan helped herself to *bara brith*, with a wedge of Caerpfilly cheese, and Annie picked up a scone.

"Later this evening," Mrs. Jervis said, "when you're ready for bed, I'll bring you our favorite nighttime treat—my daughter's special oatcakes dipped in chocolate!"

Annie nearly choked on her tea.

"I was wondering," Susan said quickly, "if you might remember back about twenty years ago a touring van with Tour Wales painted on the side. I know there were many such vans, but this one was solely owned and operated by a young man who was trying very hard to build his own business."

Mrs. Jervis looked thoughtful, and Susan decided to embellish her request. "I understand he was very popular—taking tourists to ride the little train, showing them this area's attractions. I used to know him, before he moved here, you see."

Mrs. Jervis was still thinking, trying to remember.

"He was a Welshman, of course," Susan continued, "a Llewellyn from a few miles north of here, from Llandudno."

"Oh!" Mrs. Jervis's thoughts came alive. "You must mean young David Lewellen! Tall, handsome, with dark hair and a wonderful smile?"

"Uh…"

"He was a fine one, let me tell you. Brought many a visitor here to our humble home. And he never left without one of my currant scones!"

Susan absently lifted a scone from the plate.

"Everyone liked him. Ye said ye knew him then?" Her face was aglow with curiosity.

"Well, I'm…I'm not sure we're talking about the same Llewellyn."

"Mom, show her the photo, the one in your locket," Annie suggested. Susan removed the locket, opened it and handed it to Mrs. Jervis.

Instantly, the lady's face softened into a sweet smile. "Aye, that's him all right, David Lewellen," she said. "Such a sweet boy. Do ye know what became of him? We often wondered. He was here one day and gone the next, and never a word from him since."

"No. …No, I don't know where he is," Susan said, her shoulders sagging in disappointment.

Annie injected, "Actually, we were hoping you would know. We'd like to find him. He and Mom were good friends."

"Yes, I can see that." Mrs. Jervis smiled broadly, looking at the pictures. "You were every bit as lovely back then, my dear, as you are now." Reluctantly, she handed the locket back to Susan.

"So," Annie started, "is there anyone around here who might know what happened to him?"

The lady shook her head slowly. "Can't think of anyone. And I don't know where he lived. He never talked about family. …Let's ask my daughter! Maybe she can help you." She picked up a little silver bell from the table and shook it gently, making a tinkly sound. Within minutes Miss Vanora Jervis entered, a handsome woman in her late sixties.

Miss Jervis introduced herself and apologized for not being home when Susan and Anwen arrived. "And I can't stop for tea just now, though I wish I could. I'll be accompanying the *Côr Meibion*, male choir, rehearsal this evening, and I've a lot of work to finish before then."

"Vanora is a pianist," her mother explained. "A very good one, too. She's been playing for the *Côr Meibion* for almost ten years now." She settled back into her chair. "Vanora, dear, these ladies have asked about that nice young man who brought so many guests to us years ago. You remember, David Lewellen, with his white van, the one he had to tinker with from time to time to keep it running."

"Oh, I do! Yes, a fine young man he was. And the trade worked both ways. We rang him many a time to squire our guests around."

"Would you happen to know where he went when he left Betws-y-Coed?" Susan asked.

"No, for sure an' I don't. I heard he left Wales, though. Went to Scotland, I think. Maybe it was England. Oh, I just remembered there's a pile of old brochures in the drawer over there." She started toward the sideboard. "We keep things around forever," she said, apologetically. "Hate to throw anything away, in case we might need it again someday, you know." She opened the drawer and lifted out an armful of papers. "Here, Mum," she said, depositing them on the corner of the table beside her mother. "Go through them with the ladies. I do believe one of David's fliers is in the stack." She turned to Susan and Anwen. "Please excuse me, ladies. I really must get back to my bookkeeping. Mum is an excellent hostess," she added, giving her mother a quick hug. "She'll take good care of you."

Miss Jervis disappeared into the back of the house, and Mrs. Jervis began leafing through the pile of fliers and brochures. Unfortunately, she took time to reminisce over each one, sorely trying Susan's patience. Susan looked at Annie and rolled her eyes heavenward.

"Mrs. Jervis…" Annie said. "About, uh, David's advertisement?"

"Oh, forgive me, dears! I'm just an old woman who enjoys living in the past." She quickly turned over several more papers, then lifted one and handed it to Susan with a triumphant smile. "There!" She read aloud, "Tour Wales with David Lewellen!"

It was a photocopy of a sheet of plain paper that someone with excellent penmanship had developed into an attractive flier. *Rhys/David?* Susan wondered. She read: "Offering tours to Conwy Castle, Bodnant Garden, Swallow Falls, and other points of interest in Snowdonia National Park." A phone number was listed, certainly disconnected long ago. But it was a start. Now she knew that he had changed his name to David. And he had changed the spelling of his last name.

"Could…would it be possible for me to make a copy of this?" Susan asked.

"Certainly, dear. Vanora can do it for you, back in her little office. I'll take it to her right now."

"Thank you, Mrs. Jervis. Thank you very much."

"I'll leave it by the front door so you can pick it up on your way to dinner. I expect you'll be getting ready now." She took the flier and rose from the table.

"Oh, I think we've changed our minds about having dinner," Annie said. "Haven't we, Mom?" she implored. "Your tea was lovely, Mrs. Jervis. We really don't need any more to eat!"

"In fact," Susan said, "we'd like very much to take a walk around your grounds, if you don't mind."

"Yes, please do! There's a nice footpath around the lake. There, look out the window, you'll see it."

At home, it would have been called a large farm pond, not a lake, but it was very pretty and inviting. "We'll do it. Thank you."

At the doorway, Mrs. Jervis turned suddenly. "Oh, ladies, since you won't be going out to dinner, I wonder if you might like to attend the *Côr Meibion* rehearsal with Vanora and me tonight? Visitors are always welcome at rehearsal, and we'd love for you to hear some traditional Welsh music."

Susan's eyes lit up. "You said the magic word—music!" She looked at Annie, who nodded enthusiastically. "We'd love to go!"

"Casual dress, dear. We'll meet you at the front door promptly at seven o'clock. The chapel is just a few miles east of here."

"Mrs. Jervis?" Annie asked. "Would you happen to have a computer in your office? One with Internet access?"

"Sorry, dear. No. But we do have a very nice typewriter."

Annie smiled. "Is there a place in town that might have a computer for public use?"

"Hmmm. I believe the bookshop has one." She looked at her watch. "They'll be closed now, but they open at ten o'clock in the morning. Vanora!" she called down the hall. "Doesn't the bookshop have a computer that tourists can use?"

Vanora stuck her head out of a doorway at the end of the hall. "Yes, certainly. They do charge a small fee."

Susan and Anwen thanked the ladies and headed for the stairway. Once in their room, Susan said, "A computer, Annie?"

"Yes! When Brian extended his search to all of the U.K., he turned up a David Lewellen. I remember, because I remarked on the different spelling. I want to do another search. This time I'll know what to look for!"

~ ~ ~

David Lewellen's Tour Wales had earned enough during its operation in Betws-y-Coed to pay back every pence loaned to him by Mr. Siam Whittal. After all of the troubles and accusations against him in Conwy, David had declined Mr. Whittal's offer of matched funds, opting instead for a loan. He'd wanted to prove his honesty, though there had been no need. When he made the final payment, Mr. Whittal had a proposition for him. "Go to a big city," he'd said. "Cardiff, London, Edinburgh, wherever you like, and start a *big* tour business, one that can grow branches in outlying areas and make you some real money. I'd like to fund it for you."

"No, Mr. Whittal, but thank you anyway. It's taken me a long time to pay off your loan, and now I'm ready to bank money for Brisen and myself. I have Nia to think of, too. Please know that I am very grateful to you for giving me my start. If it weren't for you...well, I hate to think where I might be now."

"Hear me out, Rhys—I'll always call you Rhys; can't get used to David— there's more to my offer. I'm getting older, my heart isn't so good any more, and I have no family. You've been like a son to me, and I've watched you grow into a responsible young man. I'm very proud of you, that you prevailed and prospered despite the troubles you've been through. When I said I want to fund your business, I meant just that—it's not a loan; it's a gift. Father to son. ...Well, what do you say?"

David was overcome with emotion. He was glad he was sitting down and in the comfort of Mr. Whittal's study. "I...I don't know what to say."

"Make an old man happy, Rhys. Say Yes. I'll help you locate office space, buy vans, hire staff. You organize everything and do the training. ...Please?"

Now, nineteen years after "proving himself," David Lewellen owned a business worth a few million British pounds. Siam Whittal's heart had finally stopped beating, but not before he had seen the results of his encouragement, the results of his unwavering faith in young Rhys Llewellyn. David smiled at the memory, which never failed to humble him. His benefactor had, indeed, been like a father to him.

How he wished he could have shared his success through the years with Susan, the love of his life. If only he hadn't been so stubborn, so hard-headed about staying clear of her. But perhaps if he hadn't been those things, he wouldn't have risen in business. He might have had Susan but not have achieved any personal pride. He could not have lived with that. Susan had achieved a great deal. He wanted her to be proud of him. Too, Brisen and Nia had needed him in the early years. They were a close threesome then and remained close now. And Brisen's husband, Kent, had become like a brother to him, even worked in the business as one of his managers. . . . Rhys Llewellyn may have been an orphan, but David Lewellen had a family. And he loved them.

He removed Susan's photo from his wallet, kissed it, and placed it on his desk, where he could see it as he checked his e-mail one last time before going home.

. . . No message. Nothing.

~   ~   ~

The *Côr Meibion* was an incredible singing group of about twenty men, one of many such choirs all over Wales. Mrs. Jervis said that sometimes the boys from Blaenau Ffestiniog joined in the rehearsals. Susan suspected that the "boys" were close to Mrs. Jervis's own age.

"It's a family tradition in these parts," Vanora Jervis explained during the drive to the church. "My uncle and my father both were in the choir. In fact, that's how I became interested in playing the piano—I listened to their rehearsals from the time I was six years old."

"It was good for you, dear," her mother said. "Much better than just sitting in front of the telly, as so many youngsters do today. The choir has such a beautiful sound." She turned to Susan and Anwen in the backseat. "The men sing with a lot of *hwyl* and *hiraeth*."

"What?"

"She means they put a lot of feeling into their singing," Vanora explained.

"Right from the heart," Mrs. Jervis added. "All amateurs, they are, but they sound so professional!"

They did, too. In addition to the expected hymns and Welsh patriotic songs, Susan and Anwen were treated to powerful renditions of "Bridge Over Troubled Water" and "When I Fall in Love." In English, of course.

"Thank you very much for inviting us!" Susan exclaimed after the rehearsal. "What a wonderful evening!"

Annie echoed her mother's words. She was very happy tonight, mostly because her mother was happy. *Tomorrow, Mom will be even happier,* Annie thought, *because I am going to locate the illusive David Lewellen!*

103

Chapter 16

Susan and Anwen were waiting outside the bookshop when it opened at ten o'clock the next morning. "We have to be first," Annie had said. "If someone else gets on the computer before we do, or if several people want to use it, it may be hours before our turn comes up."

So they waited. And as soon as the young man unlocked the door from the inside, they went in. The cubicle was up front, near the check-out desk. Annie went straight to it while Susan made arrangements with the clerk.

"What will you do first?" Susan asked, pulling a chair up beside Annie. She sat forward, on the edge. Her nerves were also on edge.

"I'll use his name plus the keyword 'Tour' and see what comes up."

There were several David Lewellens—a racecar driver, an editor, a meteorologist, a university professor and others; and, finally: David Lewellen, President/CEO, All England Tours, London. "That's him!" Annie said. "We've got him!" She quickly went to the All England Tours website, and they read the company's biography together. It was all business; nothing personal.

"It doesn't say anything about starting the company in Wales," Susan said. "Maybe this David isn't Rhys."

"He was trying to disconnect, Mom. Remember?" Annie clicked on the link, "Founder," and there was a photo of David Lewellen.

Susan gasped. It was Rhys, but older. Handsomer, stronger...better. She sat back in her chair, releasing the tension in her neck and shoulders.

"He looks like Pierce Brosnan in those James Bond movies," Annie said. "Aunt Beth will have a fit—she adores Brosnan!"

"Write down the address, please, Annie. I want to go to London. Today."

Annie did as she was told, then pulled up a map showing All England Tours' headquarters location in London's Paddington area. She printed the map, paid the clerk, and they left the bookshop.

They returned to the Jervis home to collect their backpacks and settle their bill, insisting on paying for the extra night.

"Oh, that's not necessary," Mrs. Jervis said, kindly waving it off.

"But it is. We reserved two nights, and we're paying for two nights. Our visit here was worth every penny—I mean pence."

"Too bad you can't stay the night. We're having Toad-in-the-Hole for supper, Vanora's specialty, and we'd be ever so proud if you'd join us."

"Thank you, but we really must be going. We did enjoy being with you and your daughter and going to the *Côr Meibion* rehearsal. Thank you very much!" Susan said, and she meant it.

"I wish Vanora were here to see you off, but do come back to visit us sometime."

"That would be very nice. Perhaps we will."

As soon as they were in the car with the door tightly shut, Annie squealed. "Toad-in-the-Hole! Tell me she was kidding. I know I said I'd go home looking like a toad from all this food, but I never thought I'd be offered one to eat!"

Susan laughed. "Not a toad, silly. It's pork sausages, battered and baked. Not bad, really. Usually served with cooked cabbage."

Annie shook her head. "Makes me long for a cold, crisp salad!"

After a quick stop at a petrol station, the drive to Llandudno took less than an hour. When they turned in their rental car, the attendant asked, "Any punches?"

"Huh?" came out of Annie's mouth.

"No," Susan said. "No punches. I'm a very good driver."

As they walked toward the train station, Annie asked her mother, "Punches?"

"Dents."

Annie giggled.

Mrs. Jervis had given them a train schedule. They planned to catch the 2:35 p.m. train to London's Euston Station. From there they would take the underground—the "tube"—to Paddington.

"Why not a cab?" Annie asked. "Wouldn't that be easier?"

"Scarier, maybe. I was in London two years ago, remember. One flying ride in a London taxicab was enough for me! We'll take the tube."

By the time they arrived at Euston Station, it was nearly 6:30 p.m. There was an information kiosk nearby, where they asked about accommodations close to Norfolk Square. Fortunately for them, the nice young woman not only suggested a hotel right on the Square, she also made a reservation for them.

"It's not a large, fancy hotel, mind you," the lady said, "but it's nice, and their breakfast room is lovely."

Susan thanked her. "I do love London," she said to Annie as they left the kiosk. "So easy to get around in. And people are friendly."

The ride on the tube took another twenty minutes. As they came up the stairs to the exit on Praed Street, Annie retrieved her map. "If we walk to the corner, there," she said, pointing, "we should see Norfolk Square. Our hotel overlooks it."

"Good. I'm ready to stretch out," Susan said.

"Well, believe it or not, I'm hungry."

Susan laughed. "You? Hungry?"

"Yeah. For some real food."

"What about that cold, crisp salad you mentioned earlier?"

"We skipped lunch, remember? Now I need *fuel*. I've had enough scones, brown bread and rice cakes to last a lifetime."

"Oatcakes. They were oatcakes."

"Hmmph."

They turned down London Street, passing a magazine store, a grocery, and a launderette. "Looks like a real neighborhood," Annie said, "where I can get some real food."

A few minutes later they checked into their hotel, a small bed-and-breakfast accommodation with a pleasant lobby and a welcoming staff. Their en suite room was plain, but comfortably furnished and had the basic amenities—hair dryer, toiletries, tea and coffee.

Susan headed straight for the window overlooking the Square. Through the trees she could see where Rhys's office should be on the other side, part of one long building divided into more than one business, including another small hotel similar to the one she and Annie were in. "I'm not sure which door is his," she said. "The signs over there are really tiny. And it's getting dark outside. Wish I had some binoculars."

"Now you're sounding like me. Nosy," Annie said, joining her mother at the window. "Hmmm. The building looks elegant in an old-world sort of way, all white-painted and…well, kind of classy. I believe the Brits would call those signs 'discreet,' rather than tiny."

Susan turned away from the window. "We'll figure it out in the morning."

"I'd like to call Brian later tonight," Annie said. "Allowing for the five hours difference, I should be able to catch him just about the time he gets home from the library."

"Of course. And I want to call Beth, give her an update."

"Don't forget to tell her that your Rhys-named-David looks like Pierce Brosnan."

"You're crazy. And I'm nervous. Let's go eat."

~   ~   ~

David Lewellen had put in a long day's work and didn't get away from his office until 7 p.m. It was nearly dark. Street lamps were on, and lights from local businesses glittered on the sidewalks. As he walked toward his car, he noticed two women across the Square, ascending the steps of the little bed-and-breakfast hotel. They carried backpacks. *Smart women,* he thought. *They don't want to be bothered with luggage.* In his business he'd seen people—mostly women—traveling with as many as five or six suitcases each. He could never understand why. Who needed that many clothes on vacation anyway? He slid into the driver's seat, turned the key in the ignition, and his Jaguar leaped to life with a comforting roar.

David sighed as he stopped at the traffic light. *One more disappointing day—still no response from Susan.* He felt like a jerk.

~   ~   ~

Susan and Annie pooled their dirty clothes, enough to make one small load of wash, and put them in a bag. Annie had spotted a fish-and-chips place on London Street, with a launderette next door. The hotel desk clerk had said, yes, there was an attendant at the launderette, so Annie had suggested they drop the clothes off to be washed and dried while they ate dinner. A good suggestion.

By 9 p.m. they were back in their room with satisfied stomachs and clean clothes.

"That's the only disadvantage in traveling with a backpack," Annie said. "Clothes have to be washed *en route.*"

"Small compensation for peace of mind."

"And how is your mind right now?" Annie asked. "Is it at peace?"

Susan stood at the window, looking out across the Square toward Rhys's office building. Would she ever be able to call him David? "Peace? Yes and No," she said. "I'm glad to know where he is and that he is healthy and well-established. But I'm scared to meet him face-to-face, even though I want to. More than anything." She paused. "Frankly, I'm terrified. He has a wife and at least one child that we know of. I don't want to disrupt his life or upset him in any way, Annie.

Really, I don't. I just want to see him. . . .I *need* to see him. Maybe we could just camp out here at the window tomorrow and watch for him and I could see him and I wouldn't really have to meet him or talk to him and then we could—"

"Mom! Listen to yourself! Your 'cold feet' are showing. You are not backing out now." Annie went to the window and stood beside her mother. "Just be casual, Mom. You're meeting him as an old friend. If you don't expect anything, you can't be disappointed."

Susan smiled at her daughter. "I believe I asked you this just a few days ago—how did you get to be so wise at such a young age?"

"I've had a good role model. . . .C'mon, let's make our phone calls and go to bed. Today has been very tiring, and you'll want to be rested for tomorrow, to look your best."

Susan took a deep breath and slowly let it out. "Okay. What time should we plan to visit? Any ideas?"

"I vote for a leisurely breakfast downstairs, then we'll walk across the Square in mid-morning. Sound good?"

"I accept the advice of my very wise daughter."

~ ~ ~

Anwen called Brian while Susan showered. She thought she'd have to leave a message, since it wasn't yet five o'clock in Florida; however, Brian answered on the first ring.

"I just walked in the door," he said. "Lucky for me! How are you, Anwen? How are things going?"

"Perfect! We're in London, in a hotel right across the street—well, actually across the 'square'—from his office building. He's David Lewellen, one of the names you found when we were looking for Rhys on the Internet. He owns a huge touring company." She gave him the website for All England Tours. "You can look it up, check him out."

"That's good news. I think. What's your next step?"

"Knock on his office door tomorrow morning."

"I sure hope he has a strong heart." Brian was smiling on the other end of the line, and Annie could hear it in his voice. "I miss you," he added.

"I miss you, too, Brian. We'll probably be home in a few days. Oh, by the way, I really like your country, your Wales." She told him about being in Conwy and Llandudno, about Bodnant Garden and Trefriw, and about the *Côr Meibion* rehearsal in Betws-y-Coed.

"Someday, I'd like you to see Swansea, my hometown. The author, Dylan Thomas, called it 'an ugly, lovely town.' I guess it is, in a way—it's very busy and modern in places, yet old-fashioned and beautiful in others. Right on the coast. I know you'd like it. ...Maybe I could show it to you."

"...Maybe you could." This time, Annie was smiling on her end of the line. And Brian could hear it in her voice.

~ ~ ~

They chose a window table in the below-street-level breakfast room, where they could look upward to the sidewalk at the feet of people and dogs who passed by. The room was pleasantly decorated and the breakfast buffet superb. At ten o'clock they took the stairs to the lobby level and walked across the narrow street, into the carefully tended gardens of Norfolk Square. Susan promptly sat on a park bench.

"What are you doing?" Annie asked.

"Gathering courage."

"I thought you did that at breakfast."

"I need more. ...Why don't you go on ahead and...and meet him first. Just sort of see how things are."

Anwen stared at her mother. "You're serious, aren't you?"

Susan nodded. "Very. I'll stay here and watch the birds, look at the flowers. ...Please, Annie."

"Well...okay. I'm not sure what I'll say to him."

"You'll think of something."

Anwen entered the spacious and well-lighted reception area, so different from Snowdonia Tours in Conwy. Not a bit of clutter. Yes, there were posters describing places in England, but they were artfully arranged on the walls, as if in a gallery. A young man was studying the posters, and an elderly couple sat on a small Victorian sofa reading brochures. The receptionist, an attractive woman in her forties, was on the phone, but she smiled at Annie and motioned for her to come forward. Annie heard her speak into the phone, "No, Ma'am, this is not a travel agency; it's a touring company. There's a difference, you know." Annie picked up a brochure depicting the Roman ruins at Bath, and a moment later the receptionist put down the phone and came around her desk, holding out her hand. "I'm Elizabeth Rampley," she said. "How may I help you?"

"My name is Anwen Evans. I'm from Florida in the United States, and I...uh, I would like to speak with Mr. David Lewellen, if I may."

"I'm sorry. He's not here right now, but I expect him at any moment. Are you sure there's nothing I can help you with?"

"Actually, it's personal. We have a…a mutual friend."

"Oh, in that case let me introduce you to *Miss* Lewellen. I'm sure she would love to chat with you until her father arrives."

"No, don't trouble—" But Elizabeth Rampley had moved quickly across the terrazzo floor and already was tapping on a door marked Vice President. She pulled Anwen inside.

"Miss Lewellen, this young lady is from the United States. She's a friend of your father, and I thought you might enjoy chatting with her until he arrives." She turned to Annie. "We do love American visitors here at All England Tours!"

"No, I'm not a fr—"

"Please be comfortable. I'll bring tea shortly." Elizabeth Rampley exited, closing the door behind her.

~ ~ ~

From her park bench in the Square, Susan saw Rhys Llewellyn get out of his sleek convertible and head for the office building opposite. She sucked in her breath and hugged herself tightly to keep from running to him, from calling out his name. Not until he had entered the building and closed the door behind him, did she release herself, letting out her breath in one long audible sigh. She closed her eyes. *Please, God…please help Annie say the right things so that Rhys will want to see me.…Please.*

Chapter 17

Nia came forward to greet Annie. "Please don't mind Mrs. Rampley," she said with a bright smile. "She's a bit overanxious but a very knowledgeable and loyal person." Nia shook Annie's hand. "I'm Nia Lewellen," she said. "Please sit here with me. Dad should be along in a few minutes." She indicated a large sofa that matched the small Victorian in the lobby. In front of it was a claw-foot serving table. The window opposite the sofa overlooked Norfolk Square, which added to Annie's discomfort.

As they sat, Annie looked at the young woman beside her. Nia Lewellen was beautiful—long black hair pinned up in back, smooth fair skin—like a grown-up Snow White. And all Annie could manage was her own name. "I'm Anwen Evans," she said. "Annie." *Now what?* she asked herself. *What in the world can I say to his daughter?*

Nia was encouraging, though she had a puzzled look on her face. "You're a friend of my father?"

Anwen shook her head. "No. What I told Mrs. Rampley is that your father and I have a mutual friend." She paused. "The truth is, your father and my mother were friends many years ago. I just wanted to say hello to him and...and see if he remembered her."

Nia sat back on the sofa and studied her companion. Within seconds her face relaxed, and her smile grew very bright. "You look like your mother," she said, finally.

Annie was speechless.

"I saw the picture," Nia said, explaining. "The one of your mother and my father taken on the Great Orme." Her smile was still radiant.

"You...you saw it?"

"Yes. Dad carries it in his wallet, has carried it for many years, although I didn't know anything about your mother or the picture until a few weeks ago, when Mum told me. I'm so glad you're here!"

"But…I'm confused. You said your *mother* told you? And you're glad I'm here?"

"Yes to both questions. Mum and Dad are great friends, but they've been divorced for seventeen years. I have a wonderful stepfather who works here in the business with us. He and Dad are friends too, more like brothers."

Just then Nia's door opened and David Lewellen entered. "Mrs. Rampley said someone was here to see—" He stopped, staring at the image of young Susan sitting on the sofa next to Nia—Susan, as she had looked to him all those years before.

"Dad, this is Susan's daughter!" Nia said, rising and going quickly to him. "Her name is Anwen Evans. Annie."

Annie stood, holding out her hand, and David quickly grasped it in his. "You…you look just like your mother," he said, trying to catch his breath. "Just like I remember her," he said. "Please…please do sit down." He pulled up a wing chair as the girls returned to the sofa.

"I'm sorry to intrude like this," Annie started.

"No! No, it's not an intrusion, not at all." David's heart began to pound. "How is your mother? Is she all right?" His expression was so anxious, so excited, that Annie relaxed.

"She's fine. She'd like to see you, if you…if—"

"Yes! Of course! Yes, I want to see her. I tried to contact her. I sent her an e-mail, but…"

"You sent an e-mail? When?"

"Monday afternoon."

"Oh, dear. We left the States on Sunday night, and I never thought to do a remote check while we've been away from home."

David exhaled. "That's good news, Annie; because I thought, since I hadn't heard from her, that she, uh, maybe she didn't want to hear from me."

"Nothing could be further from the truth." David Lewellen—Rhys—was one of the best-looking men Annie had ever seen, and the excitement in his eyes made him powerfully attractive. "She's been looking for you, Mr. Lewellen. She's here."

"Here?" He looked toward the door.

"Across the street. In the Square. She was reluctant to come in, sent me on ahead as a scout."

Pierce Brosnan has nothing on this guy, she thought, as David rose and hurried to the window. *No wonder Mom couldn't forget him!*

Through the window he saw his beloved Susan across the square, sitting on a park bench amidst colorful flowers, her blond hair catching the sunlight through overhanging trees. Her head was turned downward, as if she were studying the hands clasped tightly in her lap. She looked vulnerable. And even more beautiful than he remembered. He turned and quickly left the office. Nothing, now, could keep him from the love of his life!

~　　~　　~

"Susan!"

She looked up and saw him coming toward her—walking fast, then running—and she flew to meet him, her arms outstretched. He lifted her off the ground and twirled around, hugging her tightly to his body. And when he stopped, and they stood still, it seemed as if the last twenty-one years had never passed. She looked into his face, into his misty eyes…and there was the eighteen-year-old boy she'd fallen in love with so long ago.

For David, that first hug told him all he needed to know. There was no awkwardness, no tentative touch nor timid words, no uncertainty. Susan was his first and only love—his *forever* love.

~　　~　　~

Annie and Nia saw the reunion from Nia's office window. "Do you suppose your father can clear his calendar for the rest of the day?" Annie asked with a smile.

Nia laughed aloud. "More like forever!"

~　　~　　~

He started to kiss her, but she stopped him with a gentle hand on his shoulder. "Rhys, no. You're married. I shouldn't have—"

"Shhh. I'm not married. Haven't been for many years."

"…What?"

"Shhh. I'll tell you later." His kiss was slow and gentle, all the more breathtaking in its tenderness.

"I think we're being watched," Susan whispered as they stepped slightly apart. She recognized Annie's blond hair through the window across the street.

"Mmhmm." He kissed the side of her face. "Your daughter and mine. They're both happy for us." He turned toward the office window, and the faces quickly disappeared. "Let's sit here," he said, guiding her back to the park bench. "I want to look at you."

113

They sat close together and held hands, neither wanting to break the sense of touch. Finally he said, "You haven't changed a bit."

"Oh, I've changed," she said, smiling. "You just can't see it." That was true—he couldn't see it. To him, she would always be the young girl he fell in love with. "Nor can I see any difference in you, Rhys," she added.

"Well, that's one difference right there—my name is David now. I haven't been called Rhys for…well, since I left Wales. That was a couple of decades ago."

Susan looked down at their entwined hands. "I know what happened, Rhys—I mean David. I read the stories in the North Wales newspaper archives just a few weeks ago. Had them translated. I didn't mean to pry, but I…I just wanted to find you, to know that you were alive and well…and happy."

He lifted her chin in his fingers. "I have to confess to a little prying myself. I've been following your career, watching your concert schedule, looking at your photos on the Internet. You've been on my mind and in my heart for all these years, Susan. I never forgot you. …Not for one minute."

"Then why…*why* did you break my heart?"

~ ~ ~

Forrest Fletcher jogged down his long driveway—more like a road, actually—and retrieved the morning paper. He was in fairly good physical shape from workouts at the prison, when they'd allow it, and doing pushups in his cell. The morning jog hadn't winded him in the slightest. Back at the house, he stopped and waved to the caretaker, who was now coming down the driveway in his jeep, ready to start mowing. Fletch knew he had to be pleasant to that guy. Didn't want to lose him. He managed a toothy smile along with the wave and disappeared into the house.

Coffee was ready. He poured himself a cup and sat at the kitchen table, stretching the paper out in front of him. Front page was full of local crap; had to turn the pages to find anything interesting. Some business exec got caught with his hands in the till, stupid jackass. Shouldn' a got caught. *I learned that lesson*, he thought, *except I didn't really get caught—someone turned me in.* He scratched at the coarse hair already thickening on his chin and turned another page. War still going on in Iraq, just like Vietnam; can't mind our own damn business.

Then a "human interest" story caught his eye. Some guy out in Texas had kidnapped a ten-year-old boy and kept him locked up for six years. The guy's friends and neighbors had never suspected he was capable of such a thing. Fletch snickered. The reporter had interviewed a know-it-all shrink who said, "It's not unusual for this kind of perpetrator to hide his crime behind a respected cover. Kidnappers and rapists are often thought to be model citizens, the trusted next-door neighbor." Yeah. Well, Fletch had been a "model citizen," hadn't he?

Occasionally, when Fletcher thought about his mother, who ran off when he was a child before he really got to know her, he wished he could feel remorse for what he did with Susan and those other girls. He was sure his mother would have wanted that. But even during those times of introspection, he could not conjure up "proper" feelings—weepy, sad feelings. They were missing from his gene pool. That was probably his mother's fault.

She disappeared right after I found the nest of baby snakes and put it in her closet, he recalled. *Some of them got into her shoes and she didn't like it. Pops told her it was just a joke but it really wasn't. I did it on purpose because she made me mad. She wouldn't let me go to the carnival. Said she saw me catching butterflies and pulling their wings off; said it wasn't 'nice' and only nice boys could go to carnivals. If she'd let me go, I wouldn't have put the snakes in her closet. It was her own fault! She even called me 'evil'—a six-year-old boy evil? She was the evil one! She abandoned her little boy!* He'd thought about trying to find her. But then, what would he say? …Fletch wondered, briefly, if she'd ever loved him.

Again, his thoughts turned to Susan and those other girls, the need for secrecy and threats when he took them. Before that, when he was a teenager and dated pimply-faced girls, he didn't have to worry about having sex, because they all wanted to do it, especially with him. He had all he needed and more. Later, as an adult, he'd dated the "right" women to please his father and boost his own image. *What a rip-off.* Those women had clung to him, told him how handsome he was, and whined that he was all business. But when he tried talking about something other than business, like sports or movies, they wanted to talk about the "club" and parties and dances and who was there and who wasn't. *Stupid stuff!* They liked kissing and a little making-out, but they didn't want sex on the first date or sometimes even on the second. *Teasers, that's what they were.* And he didn't have time for that. They should have been grateful to him for taking them out and spending lots of money on them. *Goody-goody bitches!*

So he kept dating the bitches; however, on the side, he turned to much younger ones for what he wanted—*needed, even craved*—and threatened them not to tell, threatened them with their own reputations and those of their families. He could do that. He was important. How had he become important? By looking out for himself, for Number One, that's how. He'd done damn well for himself, too. His dad had been real proud of him, of how he'd built the crop-dusting business, become a leader in the community, dated "nice" women. Yes, Pops was proud. *Well, up until . . . Hell, Pops must have had those feelings, those desires, too. Those feelings are normal, aren't they? Wanting sex is normal, isn't it?* But Fletch had never known his dad to seek out a woman—any woman—after his mom left. *. . . Probably was a damned jerk-off.*

Fletch pushed back from the table, poured another cup of coffee and settled into the desk chair in his home office. He had hooked up the computer himself, and the ISP rep had been there and connected the service. Everything was ready. He didn't want to surf the Net, nor download music, or read jokes, or visit chat rooms. He only wanted one thing—to terrorize Susan Evans. It was payback time.

He brought up his e-mail program, chuckling to himself at his chosen identity: *Beethoven.* A musician. How appropriate!

Chapter 18

David and Susan took a cab into downtown London. With David sitting close beside her, holding her hand, Susan paid no attention to the buildings zipping by, or the traffic dodges, the near misses. The wild cab ride was nothing compared to the wild feeling in her heart. This was Rhys—*her* Rhys. David. And the emotional connection was intense. She could feel it in his touch, see it in his eyes. True, it had been intense two decades ago, but there was an innocence about them then. The innocence was gone now, and they were tuned to each other in ways not possible before.

The cabbie let them off near Westminster Bridge and they walked alongside the River Thames, across from the Houses of Parliament and away from the busy London Eye, until they found a fairly private bench overlooking the water. The only sounds were river music and the occasional flapping of pigeons' wings. At that hour of the morning, joggers had long since gone home or to work, and tourists were on the other side of the river, poking around Buckingham Palace.

So they sat there, clinging to each other, and talked, and talked...and talked. David told her about his unconsummated marriage to his friend Brisen, and swore Susan to secrecy regarding Gavin, Nia's biological father.

"But Nia thinks you're her father. Surely she'll object to my being here with you. Oh, Rhys—David—I should not have come!"

He lifted her hand and kissed it. "Nia and her mother both have been encouraging me to contact you. In fact, Nia is the one who located your e-mail address and twisted my arm until I sent the message."

"Message? What message?"

"Oh, that's right! Your daughter said you left the States on Sunday night— I sent the message Monday afternoon."

"What! What did it say?"

"You can read it tonight after you get back to your hotel. It's very noncommittal. I was afraid to intrude, even though I wanted to. After all, I knew nothing about your private life, whether you were happy or sad. And all I know now is that you have a beautiful daughter who looks just like you. Nia introduced her as Annie Evans, so I'm assuming her father is no longer in the picture."

"The man who fathered her was never in the picture." Painfully, and briefly, she told him what happened that terrible night, convincing him—and trying to convince herself—that she had put it all behind her. She did not tell him about Fletcher's release from prison.

He put his arms around her and held her closely. "I am so sorry, my darling. So very sorry you had to suffer. If I had known, I would have been there for you; but I was just a boy, wrapped up in my own troubles…afraid for you to know, afraid of what you might think of me."

"David—"

He put a finger across her lips. "All I knew about your early life was that you had advantages that I could never match, you were headed for a brilliant future; and all I could think of was that I would be in the way, I would drag you down."

"You could never drag me down. I loved you! I would have believed in you!" She pulled slightly away and looked into his eyes. "At least I had music…and you became my music. That's where I put all my love for you."

He shook his head. "I didn't know," he whispered. "I didn't know you cared that much, for so long, just as I did."

"For always." She touched the side of his face with her fingers. "I was grieving, David," she said. "My music—the beauty and simplicity of it—helped me grieve for you in a good way." She sat up a little straighter. "Since I was already a fairly good musician," she said, smiling, "letting music consume me was a natural step."

"Fairly good! You were magnificent. I remember the first time I heard you play—at the morning rehearsal for the concert in Trefriw."

Susan grinned. "Mmhmm. That's when you heard me make those mistakes you told the custodian about. What was his name?"

"Pedr." David laughed and shook his head. "You know I didn't hear mistakes—that was just an excuse. I'd heard you play 'The Gentle Bird' at rehearsal, and I was awestruck. I wanted you to play it for me—*only* me—later that night, so I told Pedr you needed to practice." He leaned over and gave her a quick kiss on the cheek. "My private concert. By then I'd already fallen in love with you. Then, when you played 'The Rose' for me, and sang the words, I was so overcome with emotion I nearly ran from the room."

"No!"

"Yes. Couldn't let you see me in tears then, could I? Me, a big strong Welshman two years older than you."

She smiled. His accent, his way of speaking, still fascinated her.

David squeezed her hand. "I'm glad you had your music to get you through the hard times," he said. "And I had a company to build. Fortunately, I had ample funding, thanks to Mr. Whittal, and strong personal support, thanks to my friend Brisen—I want you to meet her, Susan. Brisen will be so happy for us!"

"I'd like that. But why didn't you go back to Wales? It's your home."

He shook his head. "No. Not after I'd been shunned by those I'd considered friends. Wales was no longer home." She could hear a touch of bitterness in his voice, still present after so many years. "Too," he said, "Mr. Whittal encouraged me to build the company in London. More opportunities, he said. And he had connections here." David squeezed Susan's hand. "It was a good move."

Susan sighed. "I guess we both had something positive to do, something consuming. Music helped me immensely, gave me a reason for being. And after that awful encounter with Forrest Fletcher...well, music saved me. Sometimes I regret losing all those years with you, yet if not for that loss...I wouldn't have Annie. Fletcher's attack was, by far, the worst thing that ever happened to me," she said. "I'll never forget it. Yet, in some unfathomable way, I can forgive that man—that *person*—for it, because it produced the brightest light of my life—Annie. Anwen."

He smiled. "You gave her a Welsh name."

"Mmhmm. In memory of you. I thought you were lost to me forever."

He kissed her lips, as a soft breeze from the Thames lifted her hair very slightly. "You know what I think?" he asked, not expecting an answer. "I think we're the two luckiest people on Earth. We each have a daughter we love, we're both happy and successful, and now we have an opportunity to make up for all those lost years." He traced the side of her face, gently, with his fingers. "Nothing will ever come between us again."

~   ~   ~

Forrest Fletcher read through "Beethoven's" message to Susan Evans and made a few changes. Then he sat back and admired his work. Finally, with a wide grin, he pushed "Send."

~ ~ ~

David had called Nia on his cell phone as he and Susan left Norfolk Square for downtown London. "We'll be back this evening to take you both to dinner," he had said. "Be ready." Meantime, Anwen chose to do a little exploring and window-shopping in Paddington, and Nia reluctantly went back to work.

It was clear to both young women that they could quickly become friends. The rapport had been relaxed and easy.

"How long have you known?" Nia had asked. "About your mum and my dad, I mean."

"Only a few weeks."

"Same as me!"

"Yeah. Mom finally showed me what was in the locket she's worn around her neck since before I was born. I'd asked her about it many times while I was growing up, but she always put me off. This time, though, she showed me. It was the photo of the two of them at the Great Orme."

"I'll bet it's the same one Dad carries in his wallet!"

"Probably. But hers was cut apart to fit their faces into the locket."

"Soooo romantic! Can you believe they've loved each other all these years?"

"Oh yeah. The difference in my mom since we decided to look for Rhys—I mean David—is truly incredible. She absolutely shines!"

"And did you see the way he ran out of here and into the Square, and swept her up in his arms—just like in the cinema!"

"Pretty great, huh?"

"…Guess we shouldn't have been watching."

Annie giggled. "Guess not."

~ ~ ~

They dined at Pierre Victoire in Soho, enjoying the casual atmosphere and live piano music. Annie and Nia tackled the hummus, olives, and French bread that were served as they were seated, worrying David that the girls would be too full to eat the main course.

"Dad, you know me better than that," Nia said, rolling her eyes.

Susan looked at Annie and grinned, recalling her daughter's comments at being plied with food everywhere they went in Wales. "Not worried about going home looking like a toad?" she asked.

Annie wrinkled her nose at her mother and shoved another piece of bread into her mouth. It was clear that the girls enjoyed each other's company. And that made Susan very happy. And David.

"Anyone for Banoffe Pie?" the server asked, after the dinner plates had been cleared.

"What's that?" Annie asked.

"An absolutely delicious combination of bananas, toffee, and cream."

David warned the women: "A *big*, absolutely delicious combination, etcetera, etcetera."

Susan laughed. "Why don't we get one piece and four forks?"

That settled, they finished the evening on a sweet note.

~   ~   ~

After making plans to meet the next day, they said their goodbyes in Norfolk Square, and Susan and Annie mounted the steps of their hotel. Susan headed straight for the computers in the lobby alcove, while Anwen stopped at the front desk for the computer access code.

"I have to see his message," Susan had said. "I can hardly wait to see Rhys's first words to me after twenty-one years!"

"You mean David."

"David. I suppose I'll get used to that name eventually."

Annie sat at the computer and called up Susan's e-mail. There were a few messages from friends, a couple from colleagues, one from "Beethoven," whom she supposed was a musician colleague, and one from "D. Lewellen."

"That's it! D. Lewellen."

Annie clicked on the message and rose, giving the chair to her mother. "I'm going upstairs and hop in the shower, Mom. See you later." She left, allowing Susan some privacy.

~   ~   ~

The message was short:

Dear Susan,

It's been a very long time, but I'm hoping you remember me. I was that starry-eyed young man from Wales who fell in love with you, then disappeared with no explanation. I'd like to apologize and offer you, finally, that

explanation. Susan, would you allow me the opportunity? Would you reply to this message?
Sincerely,
Rhys (David Lewellen)
PS: I never forgot you.

A soft, happy sound escaped her lips and she furtively looked around, assuring herself that no one had paid attention. Susan quickly scanned the other messages, mostly of the "hope you're having a good time" variety. Last, she clicked on "Beethoven."

Dearest Sweet Susan,
Yes, the sweetest of them all. I have fond memories of our dates, particularly the time we spent together gazing at the moon over the Flint River. Well, at least I saw the moon. Such a beautiful night, such a beautiful girl. You can't imagine how much I'm looking forward to seeing you again. I want to show you my farm. You'll love the house and the fields, especially the fields. We can watch the moon rise and see the sunset across those golden fields.
Forgive me for being so poetic. It's just that you inspire me. Thoughts of you warm my blood and cause me to rise to new heights, figuratively speaking. It's nice that you're becoming famous. I'm proud of you. I'll see you soon. Until then, keep me in your thoughts. I know you will, Sweet Susan.
All my love,
Beethoven

This time, the sound that escaped her lips was neither soft nor happy. Susan fainted.

Part III
Vivace

Chapter 19

By the time Anwen arrived, after being summoned by the desk clerk, Susan was coming around, her head supported by a kind woman with a Cockney accent. "Cried out, 'er did, just afore she fainted! I was sittin' right next t'er. 'Twas somethin' on that screen got 'er all upset like." She nodded toward the computer Susan had been using.

Annie looked up at the monitor and noted that the message was from "Beethoven." Without reading it, she quickly logged off and exited the program. By then, several people had gathered, and Susan was helped to her feet.

"I'm fine," Susan assured them. "Just had a fainting spell." She forced a smile. "I probably shouldn't have skipped dinner."

Annie gritted her teeth and guided her mother to the elevator, thanking the folks for their kindness. When the doors had closed, she said, through clenched teeth, "Skipped dinner? More like too much dinner! Maybe the Banoffe Pie? When we get to our room you can tell me what *really* happened."

"My e-mail! It's still on the screen!" Susan reached toward the "down" button.

"I logged off and shut it down. Don't worry about it."

"Did you...?"

"I didn't read it."

In their room, Annie's voice was more gentle. "Are you sure you're all right, Mom? Would you like me to get you something, some juice maybe?"

"No, dear. I'm fine, probably just tired from today's excitement. A good night's sleep is all I need." She grabbed her nightgown and headed for the bathroom.

Anwen waited a few minutes, then called through the door. "And do you think you can get one? A *good* night's sleep? ...Or will you toss around all night, thinking about Beethoven?"

The door flew open. "I thought you said—"

"I didn't read it. That's true. But I saw the signature before I shut it down. That message made you faint, Mom. What was it?"

Susan straightened her nightgown and slid into bed, sitting up against the pillows. She pulled the covers up to her elbows.

Annie sat on the other bed and faced her mother. "Well? ...Who is Beethoven?"

Susan stared straight ahead, not answering.

"The message must have been pretty strong, to cause you to faint."

Susan turned to look at her daughter's loving, serious face, but still did not reply.

"Mom, are you going to treat me like the adult I am, or am I back to being a child in your eyes?"

She had stripped away Susan's defenses. "It was him," Susan said, simply. "The man who fathered you."

"What? ...I thought he was in prison."

"He was. He's out now."

"...And you knew this and didn't tell me?"

"Annie, it's nothing for you to be concerned about."

"Nothing! Nothing? His message made you pass out, Mom! What did that bastard say?"

Susan shook her head, tears forming. "It was a...it was...his obscene version of a love letter."

"A love letter! Mom, this has to be reported. Even I know that a sex offender is forbidden to contact his victims. That's the law."

Susan nodded. "When we get home, I'll report it. But maybe this is the only message he'll send. Maybe he just wanted to torment me one last time. Maybe..."

"Maybe nothing! That creep belongs back in jail, and if you don't report him, I will."

"I'll do it, Annie. As soon as we get home." She slid beneath the covers and turned to face the wall.

"Promise?"

"Promise," Susan mumbled.

~   ~   ~

Next morning Susan and Anwen once again had breakfast in the pretty breakfast room below street-level. Both were dressed comfortably for a day in

London. Nia had arranged for the day off so she could take Annie to all of the "fun" places; David, likewise, had the day off, but his only plan was to be with Susan, wherever that led.

"Are you going to tell me what that message was all about?" Annie asked, swallowing a bite of bagel.

Susan sighed. "It was a veiled threat, meant to scare me. And it did."

"Well, you need to print out a copy to keep safe, and you also need to save it in your e-mail for evidence. Do not delete it, Mom." She began peeling a banana. "I hope you aren't thinking of answering it."

"Annie! I would never communicate with that...that person!"

"I sure would like to."

"What?"

"I'd like to tell him exactly what I think of him, that he's a creep and a pervert and he should live in a hole in the ground where all snakes live."

Susan's mouth twisted into a wry smile. "No chance of that. He lives in a sprawling farmhouse on a vast amount of land, at least I assume that's where he is now. Beth told me that when his father—a nice man, incidentally—died, Fletcher resumed control of the property and the accumulated wealth. Now that he's out of prison, he's a very rich man."

"That's his name? Fletcher?"

"Yes. Forrest Fletcher. Everyone called him Fletch."

"I think Lech suits him better."

Susan couldn't help chuckling. *I am so lucky to have Annie*, she thought. *She's my sunshine in the darkness.*

"Enough of him!" Annie said, standing. "He's not worth another word. I have a big day ahead of me, and you have a big *romantic* day ahead of you."

Susan's smile grew wide and bright. "You're right; I do. Let's go!"

~   ~   ~

David helped Susan into his low-slung Jaguar. The top was down, perfect for a sunny but cool day. The Jag was the smoothest, most comfortable car Susan could ever remember riding in. The driver's side, of course, was on her right— something she liked but was sure Annie could never get used to. Annie and Nia had left a half-hour earlier for the tube station around the corner on Praed Street, and David had taken a little time to show Susan around his office. It was now late morning.

"So, where are we going?" she asked, as the cat-car purred along the street.

"It's a surprise."

"A surprise!"

"Mmhmm. Just sit back and enjoy the scenery."

As they left London via the A40, Susan read the road sign. "We're going to Oxford?" she asked.

"No, not nearly that far. Just a few kilometers."

In the past, Susan had only seen the English countryside by train. Going by car was a pleasure, and she didn't mind that David's "few kilometers" would certainly be several miles. As city scenes gave way to country, many shades of green emerged, dotted with colorful flowering trees.

"This is beautiful," Susan said. "So, where are we going? You realize the suspense is killing me!"

He laughed. "The truth?"

"Yes!"

"I want to have you all to myself today. Do you mind?"

She reached across the console and placed a hand on his shoulder. "I'd like that very much. ...Where are you taking me?"

"Well, I couldn't take you to my London flat. It's an impersonal sort of place where I stay during the week. Besides, it's cluttered as only a man can clutter."

Susan laughed. "I wouldn't mind clutter, as long as I'm with you." Her voice softened. "I mean that, Rhys. ...David."

He glanced at her and grinned. "You're distracting me," he said.

"So where are we going?"

"We're going to my permanent home, which is a country house near High Wycombe. I think you'll like it."

"An English country house!" Susan's voice betrayed her astonishment.

"It's not what you're thinking," he said quickly. "It isn't a thirty-room mansion with extensive formal gardens and a park. It's merely a nice, cozy house in the country."

Susan exhaled. "Whew! That's a relief. I don't think I'd be comfortable spending the day with a country squire or landed gentry or a baron or whatever you British people call yourselves."

David laughed. "I call myself a businessman who needs a little place to get away from business." He turned off onto a side road. A few miles later, just beyond a meadow of daisies, he turned the car into a long driveway lined with tall hedges. "We're almost there," he said.

Still, Susan couldn't see the house. "Where is it?"

"Around the next curve."

And there it was. It may not have been a thirty-room mansion, but it was a mansion nonetheless, a square-shaped stone structure with a gradually sloping roof and several tall chimneys. The landscaping around it was gorgeous. Susan could only gape.

"Do you like it?" David asked, tentatively, as he stopped the car.

She swallowed. "Oh yes! But…do you live here…by yourself?"

"For now." He turned to her with those intense black eyes and she thought she would melt. She leaned toward him, and he kissed her, once, very tenderly. "For now," he repeated.

"Let's go inside." David helped her out of the car, and they started toward the stone steps. "Actually, we won't be quite alone. Mr. and Mrs. Newbury are my live-in caretakers, but they have a way of disappearing into the woodwork when I arrive."

In fact, the Newburys met them at the door. "Welcome home, Mr. Lewellen!" they said in unison. "And welcome to your guest," added Mr. Newbury.

They stepped into the foyer and David introduced Susan. It was clear that Susan's visit was not a surprise to the Newburys. "So nice to have a famous musician in our midst!" Mrs. Newbury said, with great enthusiasm. She was short, a little on the chunky side, and her eyes twinkled.

Susan laughed. "I don't know what David's been telling you, but I am definitely not famous."

"Well, almost then," the woman said. "Tea is set in the dining room, Mr. Lewellen. We'll be off now. Going to the market at Aylesbury."

David thanked them, and they disappeared.

Susan began wandering through the unpretentious, welcoming home. The rooms, though few, were large—the foyer with a winding staircase, a living room, dining room, kitchen, library and "powder room" on the first floor. Each room had an interior doorway leading to another room, so the entire house was connected on the inside. The furnishings were casual and elegant, lacking the antiques and paintings one might expect to find in an English country house. "It's lovely," Susan said, running her hand along the polished banister. "May I see the upstairs?"

"You can see…do…be…*have*…anything you want, my darling Susan." He gestured for her to ascend the stairs.

On the second floor were large bedrooms, each with its own bath. Again, the furniture was simple, timeless. At the far end of the hall, next to the Newburys' bedroom, stairs led up to the attic, which David said was unfinished and held only a couple of trunks full of old memories.

"That explains the dormer windows I saw as we were driving up," Susan said. "Attic windows." She sighed. "This is truly beautiful, David. A dream house."

"It has never looked more beautiful than it does today. You make it complete." His smile was infectious.

Susan turned to the final doorway, which was across the landing. "Another bedroom?" she asked, walking toward it.

David nodded, and crossed in front of her. "Mine," he said, pushing the door open.

She stepped inside and was at once charmed by the room's quiet masculine beauty—shades of gray and pale green, a king-size sleigh bed and some chests of drawers to match. It took only seconds for her to notice the photo on his bedside table, yet another copy of the one taken at the Great Orme. She smiled and turned, then stopped suddenly. On the wall facing the foot of the bed was a large painting—a formal portrait...of her.

She had never seen anything like it, not even a photo or snapshot. She certainly had not posed for it. Yet there it was. Susan Evans. No mistake. She was stunned into silence.

After a few seconds she felt David behind her, his hands on her shoulders. "I commissioned it," he said quietly, "about ten years ago. It's a composite of several photos I'd gathered from American magazines, newspapers, your university's website."

"T-ten years?" she managed to say, still staring at the portrait.

He kissed the back of her head. "When I told you yesterday that I never stopped loving you, I meant it. I also told the artist that I loved you; and, as you can see, he filled your eyes with love for me. I was glad. I saw those eyes every night before I fell asleep."

She turned to him, tears of happiness spilling onto her cheeks, and he took her in his arms. This time, their kisses were not tentative, nor guarded; and within a few minutes David and Susan were together on the sleigh bed. *Really* together. Finally.

Chapter 20

"I have always loved you," he said, "but now more than ever." His fingers were entwined in her hair, and her hand lay gently across his chest. "For all these years, all I had were memories of a few stolen kisses beneath the trees in Trefriw."

"And in the car park at the Clarence Hotel," she added. "Remember when Mrs. Fleetwood found us and ushered me inside?"

"I remember." He kissed her, tenderly. "I remember everything."

She snuggled closer to him. "For years, I've felt that a big chunk of my life was missing. Now I have it back, and I'm not going to lose it again."

He grinned. "So, I'm a big chunk, am I?"

She couldn't help laughing, and playing. And then they played some more.

~   ~   ~

That evening they met Annie and Nia at La Grande Marque on Middle Temple Lane, just off the Strand in London. La Grande's elegant rooms were carpeted in burgundy; long white cloths hung from the tables, and endless choices of silverware surrounded the plates.

Annie ordered Potato Gnocchi with Broad Beans, Tomato and Pecorino Cheese. "I don't know what it is," she confessed, after the waiter had left, "but I'm sure it will be good. This place is beautiful!"

"Glad you like it," David said. "It's fairly new, within the last few years. This is Nia's first visit, too."

"But I wasn't as brave as Annie," Nia said. "I ordered steak and potatoes!"

Then Annie burst into a long, excited description of their day—sightseeing, a ride on the London Eye, shopping at Harrod's, buying souvenirs at the Blewcoat School National Trust shop on Caxton Street.

"Sounds like you might have to ship some stuff home," Susan said.

"Nah, I can carry it."

"And if she can't, I'll ship it for her," Nia offered. Annie gave her new friend a thumbs-up.

They parted around midnight, Susan and Annie to their hotel on Norfolk Square.

"I feel like I've found more than a new friend—I have a sister. I really like Nia," Annie said, lugging her packages up the front steps of the hotel. "This was one of the happiest days of my life!"

"Well it wasn't one of the happiest days of my life," Susan said.

"…It wasn't?"

"No. It was *the* happiest day! …Well, after the day you were born, Annie."

They hugged each other, then entered the lobby. "You go on upstairs, Mom," Annie said. "I'll check the e-mail real quick. Brian promised he'd write."

Susan relieved Annie of her packages and stepped onto the lift with a big smile on her face.

Annie sat down in front of the computer. She found the message from Brian, which added even more happiness to her "happiest" day. Then she logged onto her mother's account.

There were two new e-mail messages for Susan. …Both from Beethoven.

~   ~   ~

Should I, or shouldn't I? Anwen wondered. *I want to open them. I want to know what that creep has to say to my mother! Do I have the right? Or should I wait and let her read them?* She took a deep breath. Then, instead of opening the first one, she scrolled up to Beethoven's message from the night before, the one that had caused Susan to faint, the one Susan called his "obscene version of a love letter." Without another thought, Annie opened it and read it. She was appalled.

In anger, she scrolled down to the new messages and opened the first one. It said:

> Dearest Sweet Susan,
> Why haven't you responded to my first message? I really thought you'd be excited to hear from me, after all we've been to each other. However, to be honest with myself, you were a little angry with me the last time I saw you. I know you couldn't help it. You had to pretend you didn't like me. But I know better.

You loved being with me. Speaking of love, I understand that you have a beautiful daughter who is almost 19 years old. Hmmmm, sorry I've been away so long. Who does she look like?
Remember me forever,
Beethoven

The subject of the second message was "P.S." Annie read it:

Susan, dear, if you think this e-mail can be traced, think again. I learned some valuable lessons from a new friend while I was away. No one can ever prove who Beethoven really is. Other than being one of your favorite composers, of course. Ha! Ha!

Anwen printed both messages and started to log off. She hesitated, then scrolled back up to the earlier message and printed it also. Offering no apology, she would take the printouts to her mother. *I want to be there when she reads the new ones,* she told herself. *I will be there to support her!*

~ ~ ~

Susan was furious. Not with Annie, never with Annie. In fact she was glad, once again, for her daughter's love and initiative, glad Annie had opened and printed the messages. No, she was furious with Forrest Fletcher, his audacity in contacting her.

"The shameless, arrogant..."

"Say it, Mom."

"Son of a bitch! That's what he is. And I'm thinking of a lot worse things to call him, things I could not possibly say aloud. How dare he mention you, my daughter, in his nasty, snide remarks? He is *nothing* to you!"

"You're right, Mom. He is nothing to me and never will be. The point, right now, is that he's breaking the law. He is not allowed to contact you. You need to report him so they can put him back in jail."

"Why does he have to torment me now?" Susan began pacing. "Why now, when I've just found Rhys! I mean David! After more than twenty years I finally have a chance at...at love. At complete happiness. And now *this!*"

"Does David know about Fletcher?"

Susan stood still. "He knows about the rape. That's all. He doesn't know any details, and he doesn't know that Fletch is out of prison."

"Are you going to tell him?"

"No. …Yes…I don't know!" She sat down on the edge of the bed.

"I think you should."

"We need to leave London, Annie. We need to go back home. Now."

"No, we don't need to go now, but you do need to tell David."

Susan shook her head. "I can't drag him into this. He's been through enough trouble and pain. He's built a thriving business; he has an excellent reputation and a wonderful…family." She choked on her own words.

Annie sat beside her mother and spoke softly. "And all of that applies to you, too. You've been through excruciating trouble and pain, and you've become an accomplished musician. Almost famous," she added with a grin. "And you have a family. Not just me, but also Aunt Beth and Uncle Joel, Grandma and Grandpa. You didn't let that monster ruin your life the first time around. So don't let him do it now!"

A sudden clap of thunder enforced those words, and rain began pelting against the window. Susan rose and pulled the blackout curtains shut. "I won't," she said. "I won't let him control me from the comfort of his cozy, sheltered, expensive farmhouse! He thinks he's safe, but he's not safe from me. I'm going to have him put back in a cold, dreary cell to rot away!" She was energized.

"Now that's more like it. And, Mom, don't be concerned with what he said about tracing his e-mail. He's living in a dream world. Those computer techies at the FBI can find anyone, no matter how many layers of deceit they have to dig through."

"And," Susan said, "since we have printouts of his meanness, there's always 'probable cause' to search his place."

Annie smiled. "You've been watching too much *Law & Order*."

"Best show on television."

~ ~ ~

Next morning the sun rose, promising a beautiful day, most welcome after the night of rain.

"So we're meeting David and Nia for lunch. How do you want to spend the morning?" Annie asked her mother. She was just out of the shower, toweling her hair, and Susan was still in bed, facing the wall.

"Mmhmm," Susan answered.

"Mmhmm? What kind of answer is that?"

Susan rolled over and lifted herself on one elbow. "It means I want to stay in bed for a while. What time is it anyway?"

"Eight o'clock, lazy bones. Wouldn't you like to explore the neighborhood?"

"No. I'd like to explore some sleep. I didn't get much last night." She rubbed her eyes with one hand. "Have pity on your poor old mother."

"Hmmph! Poor old mother, indeed. You were fighting-mad last night. You had that fire in your eyes that said, 'Don't mess with me!'"

Susan managed a short laugh and flopped back onto the pillow. "That's why I'm tired. Why don't you explore on your own for a couple of hours."

"Okay, poor old mother, I'll have pity. I'm going to get dressed and go downstairs for some breakfast. You want me to bring you anything?"

"No. I'll wait for lunch." Susan turned again to face the wall. "Hang the privacy sign on the doorknob for me. Please," she added with a yawn.

Annie smiled. "Sure."

A few minutes later Anwen was in the breakfast room, feasting on a full English breakfast—meat, beans, tomatoes, the works—and reminding herself that she must hit the gym as soon as she got back to the States. Meantime, she'd fast-walk around the neighborhood, then spend some time on a bench in pretty Norfolk Square. She wanted to think about her budding relationship with Brian Gruffyudd. Forrest Fletcher wasn't worth thinking about.

During her walk, a display in a bookshop window caught her eye and she spent an hour browsing the shelves and, yes, making a couple of purchases. So it was nearly half-past eleven when she returned to the hotel room. The blackout curtains were wide open, letting in the late-morning sunshine; the television was tuned to the news; and Susan was dressed, splashing cologne on her shoulders.

"I booked us on a flight to Atlanta, day after tomorrow," Susan said.

"That's Monday."

"So?"

"We left home last Sunday night. We'll only have been gone a week."

"That makes us pretty darn good detectives, doesn't it?" Susan peered into the mirror, pushing a wisp of hair away from her face.

"You sure you want to leave so soon?" Annie asked, quietly.

"Leave David, you mean?" She turned to face her daughter. "Oh, I'll be back. You can count on it. There's no way I'll lose him a second time. ...We'll be back—you have a new sister to visit." She gave Annie a quick hug and moved toward the little desk. "As for returning home so quickly, I'm more than ready. I'm anxious for that Fletcher-monster to get his comeuppance!"

"*Comeuppance?* You're not old enough to use a word like comeuppance."

Susan laughed, then pointed to Anwen's corner of the closet. "You need to do some planning. I can't imagine what you're going to do with all of that stuff you bought."

"I saved room in my backpack, remember."

"Not that much room. Good thing Nia said she'd ship it for you."

"Not necessary." Annie gathered up her shopping bags and started consolidating. "Look. It all goes in one bag, and I can put the books in my pack. I'm allowed two carry-ons, so we're cool, Mom."

"Cool?"

"Yeah, it's an old expression. But not as old as comeuppance."

Laughing, Susan threw a pillow at her daughter, then picked up the phone. "I'm going to call Beth and let her know our schedule."

"Okay. I'm going downstairs. I'll meet you outside in the Square."

Chapter 21

The four of them met in Norfolk Square and walked across the street to Sawyers Arms, a popular pub. They were shown to an upstairs window-table overlooking the Square. The table was set for six.

"Six?" Susan asked.

David held the chair for her as she was seated. "Hope you don't mind," he said with a smile. "Brisen and Kent are joining us."

Susan looked up in surprise.

"I couldn't keep you a secret," he explained, "not with Nia going on and on over the phone with her mother."

"Hey!" Nia gave her father a playful poke. "It's true," she said to Susan, "but I do not apologize. Mum wants to meet you. In fact, she's been begging Dad to contact you for years."

"They ganged up on me," David said.

"Well, I'm glad they did," Susan said, smiling. "I'd love to meet her."

In just a few minutes Brisen and Kent arrived. Susan could not help admiring Brisen. She was tall, and her shiny black hair hung loosely on her shoulders. "Your beautiful daughter looks just like you," Susan said, as they were introduced.

"And you haven't changed a bit from the pretty blonde in that picture of twenty years ago!"

They started chatting immediately, entirely comfortable with each other, and soon all six were enjoying the company as well as the food. It was obvious to Susan that Brisen and Kent were very much in love. Even after many years of marriage, they exchanged tender glances and sweet gestures. She recalled, of course, David's comment, that Brisen had found the love of her life in Kent. *And now I've found mine*, she thought, leaning closer to David.

"Oh, Brisen," Susan said suddenly. "I met someone in Wales—in Trefriw.

Someone you might remember. It was at a café—I can't begin to pronounce the name of it."

"Bwyty Glanrafon?" Brisen asked.

"That's it."

"Hey!" Annie injected. "That sounds a whole lot different than I thought it would."

Brisen smiled. "Was it someone who worked there?"

"No. It was a young woman who said that many years ago you found her when she was a lost child, and you kept her safe until she was reunited with her mother."

"Oh! That would be Dilys Cadogan. I'm ashamed to say I haven't been in touch with her family since I left Wales."

"Well, she's all grown up now and has a little girl of her own. She named her daughter after you."

"…She did?"

Susan nodded. "'After that lovely lady,' she told me, 'Brisen Devenallt.'"

Brisen sighed and blinked back a tear. "I'll call her," she said. "As soon as I get back to my shop, I'll call her."

"Mum has a sign shop," Nia explained. "She does beautiful calligraphy, and other artwork too."

"Now, Nia." Brisen looked embarrassed.

"It's true," Kent said. "She's a fine artist. In fact, she has something for you, Susan."

"For me?"

"Well, just a *little* something," Brisen said. She retrieved a small package from her tote bag and handed it to Susan, who opened it quickly.

"Why, it's…" Susan looked up, her eyes wide with delight. "It's a miniature painting of David's country home! Thank you, Brisen, thank you! It's lovely. And you painted it yourself?"

Brisen nodded shyly and smiled. "I knew you'd been there, and I thought you might like it."

"Oh, I do! Thank you again!"

Kent rose. "Susan, Annie, it's been a pleasure," he said. "But Brisen and I must get back to work. We'll be leaving you now." They said their goodbyes, with hugs all around, and left the others to finish their tea.

"So what's next, Dad?" Nia asked. "Do we have to go back to work, too?"

David glanced at Susan. "She's pulling my chain," he said, with a wink. "I heard her tell Mrs. Rampley that we'd both be away until Monday morning."

"Oh, good!" Annie said. "We'll have the whole weekend together before Mom and I have to catch our flight home."

"...Home? You're leaving Monday?"

Susan nodded, concentrating on the napkin in her lap. "Yes. I have a...an appointment. But we'll be back soon—very soon. I promise."

David's smile was a bit forced. "Okay. Would you ladies like to spend the afternoon in High Wycombe? I drove the Bentley today, so there's plenty of room."

"Actually," Nia began, "I was thinking that Annie and I might take a cruise down the Thames and visit the Tower of London. Also, I checked, and tickets are still available for *The Boy Friend* at the Open Air Theatre tonight in Regent's Park. I thought Annie and I could go there, and then maybe she could spend the night at my apartment. That is...if you two would like to...uh..."

Susan smiled. If she had to bet on it, she'd bet that David was blushing, just a little.

"So you want to get rid of the old folks?" he asked, grinning. "Well, guess what—we'd *love* to go to High Wycombe by ourselves!"

And they did, though the conversation during the drive was limited to the views and the weather, making David decidedly uncomfortable. Susan had not given him a reason for her decision to leave London so quickly.

~　～　～

Again, as if on cue, Mr. and Mrs. Newbury disappeared shortly after David and Susan arrived at the country house in High Wycombe.

Sunshine and a cool breeze combined for a perfect afternoon, as they strolled through the casual gardens at Whittal-Rhys House. "I missed the sign when I was here yesterday," Susan said, "but when we drove in this afternoon, I saw it on the gate out front. It's very small."

"Discreet, you mean?"

"Yes." She smiled. "I think I know why you named your house Whittal-Rhys, but why don't you tell me."

"Easy. If it weren't for Mr. Siam Whittal, I wouldn't be here today; I want to remember him always. As for Rhys..." He sighed. "I also want to remember me, the way I was."

Susan stopped walking and put her arms around him. "I will always remember you the way you were then, and I will always love that boy. But now I love the man, David Lewellen—the same, yet different. Better."

David felt a sudden release of tension. *She still loves me.* He drew her close to his body and kissed her. "You're the only one I ever loved, Susan. Then, now, forever." He held her for several moments before they resumed their walk. "I wish you didn't have to leave London so soon," he said.

She felt a sudden lurch deep within, followed by an intense ache. David had just reminded her of something she wanted desperately to forget but could not—Forrest Fletcher. She didn't want to leave London, to leave David. "I, uh...I don't really have a choice," she said, finally. "Your gardens are beautiful," she added, trying to distract him. "The roses, these bright yellow spikes..."

"Foxtail lilies."

"All of the planting seems...well, haphazard, but it's very pretty." Her words seemed forced, even to her.

"It's called 'romantic' landscaping. Fitting, don't you think?" David squeezed her hand, leading her forward along the bordered path toward a gazebo adorned with climbing roses and clematis. Inside, he kissed her cheek and motioned to a bench.

They sat facing the far side, looking out at a small pond with a fountain in the center. The breeze, now wafting through the gazebo, carried the scent of sweet peas and lilies. Yes, it was romantic. Everything was perfect...almost.

Susan was uneasy. Thoughts of going home and of dealing with Fletcher's meanness were disrupting this nearly perfect day. Like someone poking needles into her skin, Forrest Fletcher was poking his way into her life again, this time coming between her and David. She could not let that happen. She wanted to tell David, yet she *didn't* want to.

And David sensed her mood.

"All right," he said. "Why don't you tell me about it?"

Susan looked up in shock. "T-tell you? About what?"

"About whatever has a claim on the secret part of you, the part you're not sharing with me. Something's changed, rather quickly, I might add. Just a few minutes ago, you said you would always love the old me—Rhys—and that now you love me as David. Yet, when I expressed regret at your leaving London on Monday, you got all tense. Is it the 'appointment' you have? Or is it me? ...I hate to ask, but...is there someone waiting back home?"

Susan burst into tears and buried her head in his chest. "Oh, no, no, no!" she cried. "There's no one else. Never anyone else!"

He wrapped his arms around her. "Tell me about it, sweetheart. Don't keep it inside."

Susan continued to weep, softly, for a few moments, then raised her tear-stained face. "I really hadn't planned to stay here much longer because of school. Mine and Annie's. Just a few more days, really. Truth is, my whole point in coming was to find you." She managed a small smile through her tears. "That part has made me very happy. But…but something bad has happened at home, within the last two days, and I need to take care of it before it gets worse."

"Your family? Are they all right?" he asked quickly.

"They're fine. It's…" She took a deep breath. "When we were sitting on the bench by the Thames, Thursday, remember I told you about Annie, how…how she came to be born?" David nodded. "Well, the man who fathered her—the rapist—is out of prison after nineteen years."

"But he can't hurt you now. He isn't allowed even to contact you."

"He *has* contacted me. Through e-mail. The first one Thursday night; two more last night. He's playing with my mind, David. He wants to torment me until I break, to ruin my life—just like, according to him, I ruined his."

"That's monstrous! The law can put a stop to it, can put him right back in jail."

"And that's why I'm going home on Monday. My father is a very smart attorney—it was his law firm that put that worm away in the first place. Dad will know what to do." She brushed the tears from her face. "You see?" she murmured. "You see why I have to leave soon? I can't keep worrying without taking action."

David pulled her close, his lips in her hair. "I understand, my darling. I do understand. I love you very much; and because I love you, I want to go with you so you don't have to face it alone. Would you like for me to go back to the States with you?"

"You're very sweet to offer," she said, looking up at him, "but you have a business to run, and I wouldn't want to take you away from it. I won't be alone, David. In addition to Dad, and of course Mom, my sister will be there—she's always been there for me."

"And Anwen?"

"She knows about this—she's the one who found the messages—but I won't have her involved any further. I don't want her ever to set eyes on that man."

"Your parents, your sister, your daughter," he said. "They love you, and it's wonderful you have them, but that's not the same as having someone with you who's *in love* with you. I want to be there for you, too. Nia is perfectly capable of handling our tour business. In fact, she'd like nothing better than a chance to do things her way. Do you know what she said to me just yesterday? She suggested that I go back with you for a visit when you return home."

"She did?"

"Yes. She said if I let you go alone, I wouldn't be worth tuppence around the office, not even a ha'penny."

Susan laughed. "Bold girl."

"Bold and smart. Sometimes I call her 'the mouth,' fondly of course." He kissed Susan gently on the lips. "What do you say, sweetheart? May I go with you?"

"…You'd do that for me?"

"I'd do anything for you. Anything at all."

She hugged him tightly. "I'd love for you to go home with me. I just never…I never even considered that you might. You've already done a lot, you know. You listened…and you still love me." She sighed. "I didn't want to tell you because I was afraid it would spoil this visit. More than that, I hoped I could eliminate the problem and come to you, finally, without dragging old baggage along. I guess I didn't want to trouble you with it. …But now I'm glad I did."

"Me too. I want to know everything about you—why you laugh, why you cry. I want to make you feel better, not worse because you're keeping things from me. Always let me help, if it's no more than just lending an ear. …No secrets, my love?"

"No secrets." She smiled, a real smile this time, melting her lips into his, her body into his. And the scent of sweet peas and lilies enveloped them.

~ ~ ~

At dinnertime the Newburys still had not returned. Susan asked about them as David pulled covered dishes out of the refrigerator. "Oh, they'll not be back 'til the morning," he answered, casually. His accent, she noticed, became more Welsh than English when he was in the country. "But never fear," he continued. "Mrs. Newbury prepared everything in advance. All we have to do is heat it. See?" He was grinning.

Susan leaned across the kitchen's island counter. "You mean this was a conspiracy?" she asked, teasing. "The whole day was planned?"

"Actually the whole night. The Newburys asked if they could stay the night with her sister in the village."

Susan chuckled. "Sure they did."

"We're eating in the dining room," he said. "Since I'm 'cooking,' would you light the candles?" He winked at her, and she melted. Again.

Later that night, they sat on the floor in front of the fireplace, their backs leaning against the front of the sofa, their hands entwined. The fire was low-burning; the wine was a delicious cabernet sauvignon; and the music—much to Susan's surprise—was her own CD. "I've had it for a while now," David said. "Since it was first released."

Susan shook her head. "I still can't get over it. I'm so amazed that you thought about me during all those years."

"Correction. I *loved* you during all those years." He drew her close and kissed her, softly and deeply. "I guess this is as good a time as any," he said. "I'm already on the floor. Can't get much lower." He reached for her other hand; and, holding both of her hands in his, he asked, "Darling Susan, will you marry me?"

There was only one possible answer.

Chapter 22

Forrest Fletcher was disappointed that Susan hadn't responded to his e-mail. He thought she had more spunk than that. He thought she'd fight right back at him, mad as hell. Then he'd really give it to her. Or, maybe she was scared. Maybe that Miss High-and-Mighty fancy guitar-playing smart-ass who sent him to prison was running scared. He grinned at the thought. He liked that idea. That was even better than a good fight. Scare the pants off her. . . . And *that* thought made him laugh aloud.

~ ~ ~

Annie and Nia slept late on Sunday morning. Nia toasted some bagels and made coffee for Annie, tea for herself. Then Annie asked if she could use Nia's personal computer to check her e-mail. She was hoping for another letter from Brian.

"Of course!" Nia replied. "Help yourself. We're sisters now."

In just a few seconds, she was logged on.

> Dear Anwen,
>   It's only been a week, but it seems like a year! I never dreamed I could miss anyone as much as I miss you!

She read on. There were several paragraphs, some about school, a few lines about his friends and family, but Annie savored those first two sentences. And the one at the end of the next paragraph:

> I checked David Lewellen's All England Tours website, as you suggested, plus a few

other sites that discuss him and his
business. Must say, I was quite impressed. If
what I read about him is true, he is top-notch
in every way. I'm glad you found him, but
please hurry home now. I not only miss you, I,
well, I'd rather say those last two words in
person.

Anwen's heart did a happy flip-flop. Yes, she was definitely in love!

"Must be good news," Nia said, grinning. "That's quite a look on your face."
At Annie's surprise, Nia threw her hands up in defense. "Hey, don't mind me!"
she said, her grin even wider. "I'm off to the shower." And she headed for the
bathroom.

Annie was so absorbed—enthralled—with Brian's hint of love that she nearly
forgot to check her mother's e-mail. When she did, she was greatly relieved.
There was nothing from Beethoven. Not one word.

~ ~ ~

At Whittal-Rhys House, David and Susan also slept late; or, rather, stayed in
bed late. By the time they were up, had eaten a couple of scones, showered and
dressed, it was 13:00.

"What time did you say?" Susan asked.

"Thirteen hundred. Actually, ten past."

Her mind did a quick calculation. "Oh, you mean ten minutes after one
o'clock."

"If you say so." He kissed her on the forehead, then stepped back. "What
would you like to do today? Any place special you'd like to go?"

She shook her head. "What I'd really like is to stay here with you. Forever."

"Ahhh. That sounds nice. But we're both going to Tallahassee, Florida,
tomorrow. I'm booked on your flight, as of a few minutes ago. Come here,
sweetheart," he said, leading her to the window seat in the alcove. "I have a
present for you." They sat, and David took a small box from his pocket. "I
bought it yesterday morning, because I wanted you to have something more than
an old photograph to keep with you. Now, after last night, I suppose you could
call it an engagement ring, until we can get you a proper one, that is."

Susan opened the box and was immediately awe-struck. Inside was a wide,
white-gold band with six rose-gold inlay starbursts all around. And in the center

of each starburst was a sparkling diamond in a platinum setting. She had never in her life seen a more beautiful ring.

Finally, she let out the breath she'd been holding. "Rhys…thank you. It's…it's beautiful!"

"No," he said. "It's pretty. *You're* beautiful."

She threw her arms around him and held tight. "I love you!" she cried.

"And you know I love you. Now put the ring on," he chided. "It's meant to be a right-hand ring."

"No way. I'm putting it on the left, and don't you dare go looking for a 'proper' ring—*this* is my engagement ring!" She put it on and stretched her hand out in front of her eyes, turning it one way and another, admiring the ring. Then she stood and twirled around, holding her hand out to him. He looked at the ring, and at her, and even he was lost for words.

~   ~   ~

At 14:05—five minutes past two o'clock—Nia's cell phone rang and she looked at the caller ID. "Hello, Dad," she said. "What's going on?"

"Just checking to see if you and Annie are all right."

"You know we are. What do you *really* want?"

"Where are you?"

"Still at the apartment, but we're leaving in a few minutes for the Crypt. How's High Wycombe?"

He ignored the question. "We've just arrived back in London. Mind if we join you? I assume you're going for a late lunch."

"That would be great! Uh, have you two got news for us?"

"Later." He closed the phone and laid it on the car seat beside him. "Kids!" he said to Susan. "They know something's up."

"Of course they do. They're not really kids any more, David."

He sighed. "Guess not. We're meeting them for lunch at the Crypt."

"The *what?*"

"The Café in the Crypt. It's at St. Martin's, Trafalgar Square. Popular lunch place."

"St. Martin-in-the-Fields?"

"The very same."

"Rhys Llewellyn…*David* Lewellen…you keep coming up with one great idea after another!"

"Blame this one on Nia."

"I'm serious! St. Martin's chamber orchestra—The Academy of St. Martin-in-the-Fields—was on tour last year and they came to Tallahassee. Honestly, they are among the best such groups in the world!"

"Well, now you're going to eat lunch in their crypt."

Lunch in a crypt, she thought. *Oh boy*. But she was smiling.

~ ~ ~

Much to Susan's relief, this particular crypt did not in any way resemble a burial chamber. It was a spacious, below-ground café offering a variety of salads, meat and fish dishes, soups, and sandwiches.

Annie talked excitedly about the places Nia had taken her and the musical they'd seen at the Open Air Theatre. She went on and on.

"You didn't mention shopping," Susan said, interrupting, taking another bite of her sandwich.

"No shopping," Annie replied. "This time I was a true tourist, soaking up London's history and loving every minute!"

When Annie's exuberance finally wound down, Nia turned to her father. "So…Dad?"

"What?"

"You know what."

He feigned innocence. "No, I don't."

Nia rolled her eyes. "Well, Annie's been too excited to notice, but I saw it immediately."

"Saw what?" Annie asked.

Susan reached into her lap for her napkin.

"Come on, Susan!" Nia said. "Put that hand back on the table!"

She did. Slowly. And Annie's eyes and mouth popped opened. "Oooooo, wow! Let me see," she said, reaching for her mother's hand, where the new ring sparkled brilliantly. "It's gorgeous!" She looked up. "Does this mean it's official?"

"It's official," David replied. He put his arm around Susan's shoulders, giving her a squeeze. "I'm a very lucky guy."

"We're both lucky," Susan said, beaming.

Nia turned to Annie. "You know what this means for us, don't you?"

"…Yeah, I do!"

"We'll *really* be sisters."

"Officially!" And they "high-fived" each other.

~   ~   ~

By the time their very late lunch was finished, it was nearly 3:30 p.m., and the girls went off on their own.

As long as they were in the area, David thought Susan might like a ride on the London Eye, way above the city. Like it? She loved it! Afterward, they went to his office suite at Norfolk Square. Being Sunday, the office was closed and empty, so he could show her around undisturbed. He was interested in showing her the building, the other offices, the way the company worked. She was more interested in the certificates, citations, and framed newspaper clippings on the walls.

"Elizabeth Rampley's idea," he said, shrugging, "my office manager. It's a bit embarrassing."

"Why should you be embarrassed? You should be proud! I'm very proud of you, Rhys....I mean, David." She slapped herself on the head. "Now I'm the one who's embarrassed."

"Don't be." He took her in his arms and kissed her, very sweetly. "You may certainly call me Rhys if you're more comfortable with it."

"That's the way I've remembered you for twenty-one years. It still feels right, natural, to me. I have to concentrate on saying David. ...I have an idea. Would you mind if I call you Rhys when we're together in private, and try to call you David when we're with other people?"

"I'd like that."

They were in his personal office now, his desk and work area on the left, a casual area with oversized sofa and tea table on the right. He led her across the oriental carpet to the sofa, turned on the soft light of a corner lamp, and extinguished the fluorescent work lights. Susan sat on the comfy sofa, leaning back into it, and removed her shoes.

"Is that all you're going to remove?" he asked, softly.

~   ~   ~

It was dark when they left the office and crossed the street into Norfolk Square. No moon, no stars, just the glow of street lamps and the twinkle of window lights all around. They stopped on the footpath, arms around each other, and Susan said, "Could this be *déjà vu*?" She was looking across the square, toward the little hotel where she and Annie were staying.

"I was thinking the same thing," David replied. "Twenty-one years ago we stood across from the Clarence Hotel in Llandudno, saying goodbye. I was trying to be such a man, strong."

"And I was trying not to cry. We were so innocent then…Rhys." She let the tears slide silently down her face, unashamed. He kissed them away.

"But this time it's not goodbye for twenty-one years," he said. "Just for the night. I'll pack a bag and pick you up here at your hotel early tomorrow morning. You are my heart, my soul…my life! I won't lose you a second time, Susan."

Rhys remained in the square, watching until Susan was safely inside her hotel. Despite her bravery, he worried for her. Worried about her.

Susan paused in the lobby, then turned to the computer alcove. *I need to send a quick message to Beth*, she thought, *to let her know we're on our way home*. She sat in front of the keyboard and logged on. And a message popped up. From Beethoven.

Oh, no, not him again! She punched it open—not in fear, but with tough determination.

> You haven't answered my messages, Susan. I was disappointed until I just now learned that you're out of the country. Busy, busy. Going here, going there, as if you hadn't a care in the world. How did I discover you were away? Chat rooms are fun. Did you know that your friends and fans talk about you in chat rooms? You ought to try it sometime. Hurry home, Susan. We'll chat together. Ha ha! Can't wait to see you.
> Beethoven

Doesn't matter what he says. He can't touch me now. Forrest Fletcher is finished! She allowed herself a sly smile at the unexpected alliteration. *My new mantra*, she thought. *Forrest Fletcher Is Finished!*

She sent a note to Beth and started to log off, then stopped and re-read Beethoven's message. Remembering what Annie said about keeping copies, she printed it and tucked the copy into her purse. Then, on impulse, she clicked "Reply" and entered: Forrest Fletcher Is Finished!

She clicked "Send."

Chapter 23

The flight to Atlanta was smooth; and, after changing planes there, Susan, Annie and Rhys arrived in Tallahassee at 5 p.m., gaining five hours while "crossing the pond." Beth met them at the airport.

"Oh my god!" she cried, staring at Rhys. "It's Pierce Brosnan!" They all laughed, including Rhys, who was definitely embarrassed. "I had no clue you were bringing him with you Susan. What a treat to finally meet you, Rhys!"

"It's a pleasure meeting Susan's favorite sister," he said, giving her a quick hug.

"Ooo, I like the way he sounds, too!" Beth squealed. "Actually, I'm her *only* sister."

"I know. But you're still her favorite."

"You two are having way too much fun," Susan said, as Rhys put their luggage—two backpacks and his small case—into the trunk of Beth's car. "I'm exhausted."

"Jet lag," Beth said. "Now aren't you glad you left your car at my house? I knew you'd be tired after that long flight."

"Yeah, but I wish we could drive to Davenport right now and get Dad started on these e-mail messages."

"It will keep until tomorrow. Does he know you're coming?" Beth asked. "Does he know Rhys is with you?"

Susan shook her head. "No to both questions. Annie and I sent him and Mom a postcard from Wales, just saying we were having a great time, see you soon, that kind of thing. They probably haven't even got it yet. But they knew our return was open-ended."

"So why don't you call them tonight and say you'd like to visit tomorrow to tell them about your trip, maybe suggest spending the night with them. You could tell them about Fletcher's harassment after you get there. Mom would want to know too. She's not the type to be sheltered, you know."

"Maybe I should just go to Dad's office. Maybe I should make an appointment with him."

Beth laughed. "I doubt if even you could get an appointment on this short notice. He's swamped, really. Home is better."

"Yeah, I keep thinking of him as 'good old Dad,' not the busy attorney."

"Meantime, the three of you are going home with me for an early dinner. Afterward, I'll take y'all to your place and you can tuck yourselves into bed."

"Dinner?" Annie asked. "Great! I'm starved!"

"You?" Susan said. "You're the one who was so worried about coming home looking like a toad!"

"Yeah, that was me." Annie sighed, but she was smiling. "I'll start my diet tomorrow. Who's cooking, Aunt Beth?"

"Already cooked. Marlena threw something into the crockpot this morning. I haven't a clue what it is, but it has smelled wonderful all afternoon."

Annie's cousin, Marlena, was at the house when they arrived, and her uncle Joel came in shortly after, giving Rhys a warm welcome. Dinner not only smelled wonderful, it tasted wonderful! The "girls" talked about their trip, the places they'd been and things they'd seen; and Rhys answered questions about his tour business. Beth and Joel had known of Susan's twenty-one-year longing for Rhys, but Marlena had not. She was fascinated by the story, and Susan found that she enjoyed telling it. "Getting together again was so…so natural," she said. "There wasn't the awkwardness one normally feels on a first date."

"Technically, we were strangers," Rhys explained, "because so many years had passed; yet we weren't. The history was all there, and we could draw on it. It's quite wonderful," he added, squeezing Susan's hand under the table.

"Mom," Annie said, "show them your hand."

"My hand?"

Annie rolled her eyes heavenward. "Your left hand!"

With a smile she couldn't contain, Susan lifted her hand and wiggled her ring finger.

"Oooo! How did I miss that?" Beth jumped up from the table and gave her sister a hug. "Congratulations, best wishes, and all that good stuff! I am sooo happy for you both!"

"We're all happy for you, Susan," Joel added. "Congratulations, Rhys."

Susan did call her parents from Beth's house and made arrangements for the next day. When they were ready to leave, it was still fairly early. "All you travelers can be sound asleep by ten o'clock," Beth said.

"Not me," Annie said, smiling. "I'm going to call Brian, and we'll have a long, long conversation."

"She's in love," Susan explained, "and she's young. I'm in love, too, but I will definitely be asleep before ten o'clock!" Her eyelids felt very heavy. "Thanks for everything, Sis. I owe you."

~   ~   ~

"My parents don't know about you, Rhys," Susan said, when they were together in bed later that night. "I never told them. You were my special secret."

He kissed her forehead. "And how long will you keep your secret?"

"I'll keep *you* forever. The secret will be out tomorrow afternoon when my mother meets you. Dad will find out when he gets home from the office."

"I'm not sure that 'springing' me on them is a good idea."

"I love you, and I want you with me."

"And I want to be with you. But I think you need to talk with your parents before they meet me."

"I don't see how that's possible."

"Why don't I drive with you to…where is it?"

"Davenport, Georgia. It's between Albany and Americus, a little over two hours from here."

"To Davenport. I'll drop you off at your parents' home and I'll explore the town for a couple of hours while you talk with your mom. You can call me—I'll keep your cell phone—and let me know when the coast is clear."

Susan laughed. "The 'coast is clear'? Have you been reading spy novels?"

"No. For the last several years I've been listening to American tourists talk. So…is that a good plan?"

"Good plan. Now, come over here. …Closer."

~   ~   ~

Tom and Charlotte Evans had a lovely home on five acres of land just outside the city limits, and Rhys dropped Susan off there in mid-afternoon, allowing her a couple of hours with her mom before Tom arrived from work and Rhys would return to the house. The Evanses had nice neighbors—not too close, not too far—lots of birds and, of course, squirrels. Sometimes they saw rabbits and deer, more often during the past few months. They loved their home of forty years. Now, though, they were talking of moving to the city.

"But you've been here so long! It's your home, Mom. It's where you lived when I was born. And don't tell me you need to 'downsize.' You can afford the upkeep on this beautiful place."

"We're calling it downsizing, but that's not exactly true," Charlotte said. "Truth is, housing developments are going up all around us—you saw the one just down the road, and more are being planned." She sighed. "Your father and I feel sort of like the animals do—lost, uprooted, nowhere to go but out."

"Where is 'out'? Where will you go? I just can't imagine you and Dad in an apartment or condo."

"Oh, no. We're looking at homes in the city limits. Established neighborhoods. We thought if we have to be in a city—and the city *is* coming out here to us—we'd rather be in the real one, the one we're familiar with."

They were sitting side by side on a comfortable sofa in the TV room. The living room, which Charlotte had always called the 'parlor,' was filled with antiques, mostly Victorian, and couldn't exactly be described as comfortable. Susan patted her mother's hand. "I do understand," she said. "It makes me sad, but I understand." That cozy, welcoming house—which was truly a "home"— had been Susan's refuge during Forrest Fletcher's trial, a safe haven. And she would miss it.

"Now tell me about your trip," Charlotte said. "A visit to London makes perfect sense—so much to see and do—but why did you chose to begin your vacation in Wales? Of course, I know you were there as a child. Was that it?"

Susan smiled. "I wasn't exactly a child, Mom. I was sixteen. And, yes, I wanted to visit places I'd been before."

"And? . . . There's more, isn't there?"

Susan nodded. She unclasped the locket and handed it to her mother.

Charlotte fondled it, smiling at the memory. "Your father gave this to you for your sixteenth birthday. Very pretty. You've always worn it."

"Open it."

Charlotte opened it. "Oh, my! I haven't seen these photographs before. Who is that handsome boy?"

"His name is Rhys Llewellyn. Those photos were actually together in one shot. I cut it apart. It was taken at the top of the Great Orme, a mountain in Wales."

"A Welsh boy?" Charlotte looked more closely at the photos. "Hmmm. Looks to me like you know him pretty well, Susan. What was going on in Wales that summer?" she asked, a tiny smile at the corners of her mouth.

"He was our guide for the entire time; and, yes, Mrs. Fleetwood kept a stern eye on all of us. As best she could," Susan added, grinning. "Don't worry, Mom. Nothing was 'going on' other than a few stolen kisses. But that was enough. We fell in love."

"And you didn't tell me?"

"No. It was sort of like a wonderful secret. I wanted to keep it all to myself."

"Those letters you received from Wales right after you came home—they were from this boy?"

"Mmhmm."

"I thought they were from some nice little girl you met there. ...Susan!" Charlotte's smile was broader now. "You went to Wales last week to see this boy!"

"There's more to it, Mom. We lost touch over the years. Something...something happened that forced him to stop writing to me. Actually, I went there to *find* him."

"Did you? Find him, I mean?"

"Yes."

Her mother leaned against the back of the sofa. "I wondered why you never took any of your dates seriously, why you turned down that nice Steven Anderson who asked you to marry him." She held the locket up close and peered at the picture again. "All these years you were pining for this boy!"

Susan laughed aloud. "Pining! Someone in London used that very word to describe the way David dreamed of me for twenty-one years."

"David? I thought you said his name was Rhys."

And Susan told her mom the whole story. It took another hour.

~ ~ ~

Two phone calls were made: Susan called Rhys and told him that the coast was clear. And a few minutes later, after Rhys arrived, Charlotte called Tom and told him that Susan had a "beau" with her, that he was an absolutely delightful Welshman, and that the two of them would be staying for dinner and spending the night.

"What? A Welshman? She brought a stranger home from Europe?"

"Not exactly, dear. I'll explain when you get here. Be nice."

"Spending the night?"

Charlotte giggled. "We do have two guest rooms, Tom," she said.

~ ~ ~

That evening, after eating Charlotte's meatloaf, roasted potatoes, home-canned green beans, and fried apples, the four of them settled in the TV room with coffee and dessert. By then, Tom had heard the story of Rhys and Susan's meeting twenty-one years before and again recently. "It's amazing that you two

154

got together again after all these years. And that you still like each other," he added with a laugh.

"The word, Tom, is love," Charlotte said. "I think it's so sweet!"

They talked about Wales and England and the business Rhys had built from the ground up. After Tom asked a few lawyerly questions, Charlotte admonished him not to grill his future son-in-law.

"Son-in-law?"

Susan held out her ring finger, and Tom chuckled. "Okay, kids, forgive me," he said. He turned to Rhys. "I know she's a grown woman, but I still feel protective. She's had...well, some trouble in her life."

"He knows about Fletcher, Dad," Susan said.

Tom sighed. "Did you know that Fletcher's back home on his farm?"

"Oh yes. I've been dreading his release for quite a while."

"Well, he shouldn't be a problem for you or anyone else. He's being very closely monitored."

"Not closely enough, I'm afraid." Susan retrieved the copies of Beethoven's messages from her purse and handed them to her father. "This is the 'concern' I mentioned when I called you from Beth's house. There's no doubt in my mind who Beethoven is."

Tom read them. "Damn," he said, finally. "I thought that boy was rehabilitated. What a waste of brains and talent. And now he's going to find himself right back in prison."

"You know his mother ran off when he was about six years old," Charlotte said.

"Yes, and that's no excuse," Tom replied. "Harold Fletcher was a good father to that boy. Gave him everything he needed and most of what he wanted."

"Maybe that was the problem."

Tom shook his head. "No. Harold was there for him. Got him involved in Little League baseball, took him to Scouts and church, got him lessons on that guitar he was interested in for a while."

Charlotte asked to read the messages. "When did you receive these?" she asked.

"When we were in London. Annie retrieved them for me."

"She knows about Fletcher?"

"She's known about him for a long time. She just didn't know about his release."

"Why, this is terrible for both of you!" Charlotte exclaimed. "It's harassment! Tom, you can do something about it, can't you?"

"Let me see those again." He re-read them. "Fletcher was smart enough not to plant clues to his identity, nothing to tie him to you, specifically, Susan. Except maybe this line asking who Annie looks like. There's nothing here that he couldn't deny he wrote. However," he cleared his throat in his familiar, fatherly way, "this e-mail can be traced, but I'll need the electronic versions. Susan, when you get home, forward them to me at the office. All of them. Meantime, I'll keep these." He laid them carefully on the coffee table.

"But he says the messages can't be traced to him."

"He's wrong."

Susan wasn't so sure. Forrest Fletcher had spent the first thirty years of his life outsmarting everyone. She didn't believe for a minute that he'd been idle in prison. If he said he'd found a way to hide his identity, then he had. *He's still outsmarting everyone*, she thought. *No doubt about it.*

~ ~ ~

As planned, Susan and Rhys spent the night with her parents—separate guest rooms—and returned to Tallahassee the next morning, arriving around 10 o'clock. Annie had made coffee and had just poured a cup for herself. "It's good coffee," she said to her mother, "not like that mud we got in Europe. Want some?"

"Sure. You know, it's not the Brits' fault they can't make coffee. They prefer tea."

"True," Rhys said. "Coffee is an afterthought."

"No kidding. I think we have some tea bags somewhere." Annie started rummaging in the cupboard.

"I don't think so," Rhys said, grinning. "Thanks anyway."

"There are some bagels over by the toaster," she offered.

"I'll take one with me to my room," Susan said. "Your grandfather wants Beethoven's messages forwarded to his law office, and I want to do it right away." She toasted a bagel and took it, along with her coffee, to her bedroom, where her PC was conveniently located at a corner desk. She turned it on, pulled up her e-mail program and waited. ...But something wasn't right. All of her e-mail was exactly where it was supposed to be...but not one message from Beethoven.

"Annie! Rhys!" she called out. "Come here quick and help me!"

"What is it?" Rhys appeared in the doorway.

"His messages aren't here!"

"I can't help you," Rhys said, stepping inside. "I only know computer basics."

Annie rushed into the bedroom, took her mother's place at the desk and tapped a few keys. "Oh, shit."

"What? What is it?"

She fired off another expletive and looked up, her eyes angry. "Mom... He's hacked into your e-mail."

Chapter 24

Forrest Fletcher couldn't let go of the delicious thought he'd had earlier: *Scaring Susan.* Now, since receiving her nasty message, "Forrest Fletcher Is Finished," the thought was quickly becoming an obsession. She'd made him mad. Damn mad!

Snooty bitch! Thought she could track his e-mail, did she? Well, she couldn't. But he'd made double-sure. He'd hacked his messages right out of her computer system. She couldn't prove it was him now. Couldn't prove a damn thing!

He'd had nineteen years to think about what she'd done to him. If it hadn't been for her, he'd still be an important man. He'd still be on the city council, would even have served as chairman, probably more than once. He'd still be looked up to as a churchman, would be singing in the choir. Hell, he might even be teaching Sunday School! He snickered briefly, then his eyes narrowed as he refocused. Susan Evans had ruined everything. If it hadn't been for her, no one would ever have known about his "personal" life. If it hadn't been for her, those other girls would never have come forward. He shouldn't have deliberately pursued Susan that night, shouldn't have specifically chosen her. *No!!* a voice screamed in his brain. *It wasn't your fault! She was the one who started it all, the one the other girls looked up to, followed after like little puppy dogs. They said she gave them courage!* He sneered at the thought. *Huh! Susan Evans just had to blab, couldn't keep her mouth shut. Damned know-it-all ruined my life! . . . Twice! . . .* And she would pay for it.

Fletcher grabbed his gear and stormed out to the hangar where his last remaining crop-duster was parked. He'd flown it yesterday, over his own 1200-hundred acres, just to see if he still could. Of course he could! A little rusty maybe, but with some practice it wouldn't be long before he was back in shape—skimming treetops, defying electric power lines, and shaving the wool off sheep.

What he'd really like to do was fly over Snooty Susan's house and skim her roof—*that* would scare her. Better yet, he'd like to put her in a field and chase her with his plane, real low to the ground. Buzz her butt! This time his snicker turned to a howling laugh. . . . Then it became, simply, a howl.

~ ~ ~

"He's hacked into my e-mail?" Susan sank into the nearest chair, her knees wobbly. "But now we can't forward the messages to Dad's office. He needs them in electronic form!" Susan felt both defeated and angry. "Fletcher said we wouldn't be able to trace him. He's just too smart. We'll never prove he sent those creepy messages!"

"That's not true. He can be found, but by the time Grandpa's office sends the information to law enforcement, and they move it through their channels, it will take a lot longer than you'll want to wait. Longer than *I'll* want to wait. This really pisses me off!"

"Annie!"

"Okay. It *upsets* me. But don't worry, Mom. We're not screwed."

"Annie!"

Anwen stood quickly, gave her mom a hug, and started for the door. "Call Grandpa's office now, tell him what happened, and have him fax those messages to Brian at the library. The number's on that list I taped to the fridge."

"But what can you do?"

"The messages have headers on them. And that man—*Lech*—is not the only one who's computer savvy! I have some ideas of my own." She grabbed her car keys and opened the front door. "Call Grandpa!" she yelled.

Annie pulled out her cell phone and called Brian as she drove, updating him and asking him to watch for the faxes.

"I couldn't think of another place, real quick, that had a fax machine," she said. "I'm sorry to bother you, but—"

"Hey, I'll catch them. Don't worry. And don't apologize to me, Anwen. Not ever. . . . We're beyond that."

She could feel his sweet smile over the phone line.

~ ~ ~

Susan called her father and explained the problem: No electronic versions of Beethoven's e-mail.

"Virginia is faxing the messages to the number you gave me, as we speak," Tom said, referring to his assistant. "She's also sending them to my contact at the Georgia Bureau of Investigation. Those GBI boys will get on it right away, I'm sure."

"I don't know what Annie has in mind, Dad, but you know her, once she gets an idea in her head she doesn't let go."

Tom chuckled. "She's a good girl, Susan. You've done a fine job with her. I'm just sorry she has to get mixed up in this Fletcher business. I still can't believe he's done this—blatantly ignored the terms of his release."

"He ignores rules because he's sure he won't get caught. That's the way it was nineteen years ago, and that's the way it is now. He's a smart-ass."

"But not *really* smart. Sending those 'Beethoven' messages was a stupid move. We'll get him, honey. Don't worry."

"Thanks, Dad."

~ ~ ~

Anwen met Brian outside the library, retrieved the fax sheets and tucked them into her bag.

"What's your plan?" Brian asked.

"First, I'm going to trace the source information in the headers. He probably used an anonymizer, but those things aren't foolproof."

"Right. And if he's living with a false sense of security, he will likely have been careless and left traces on the intermediate hops. Would you like me to check out the chat rooms?"

"Yes! I'd forgotten he mentioned chat rooms," Annie said.

"Specifically, he said he learned about your mother's trip to Europe through the chats. If he took part in some of those discussions, we might find him that way."

"Perfect. I'd love the help! Thank you!" She gave him a quick kiss and headed for her car.

~ ~ ~

That evening, Anwen was still hunched over her laptop when Brian called. "I found Fletcher in the chat rooms," he said.

"You didn't!" Annie let out such a squeal that both Susan and Rhys came hurrying to the doorway.

"I know it's him," Brian continued, "but he doesn't call himself Beethoven, so it may be a dead end for us. He seems to be having great fun posting negative comments about your mom every time someone else posts a compliment. Listen to this: 'Susan Evans isn't half as talented as you think she is. Anyone who's had a few lessons could play faster and better.' Then someone responds: 'Faster is not better! Ms. Evans is a real musician. Her technique is flawless and, best of all, she plays with feeling. She's inspired.' His answer: 'Feeling? She has no feelings. She doesn't care about anyone but herself!' After that, other people enter and ask 'Dusty' to leave."

"Dusty? He calls himself *Dusty*?" Annie looked inquiringly at Susan.

"Of course!" Susan said, stepping into the room. "He was a crop-duster pilot. Owned a business, flew planes. 'Dusty' would be an appropriate name for him."

"And a clue for us. Brian, did you hear that?"

"I did. I'll work some more on this—follow Dusty's trail—and let you know what I find."

"Thanks, Brian. You're a love."

After Annie hung up the phone, Susan asked, "What about you? Any luck?"

"Not yet, but I'm not giving up. Beethoven is out there, and I'm going to find him."

"It's late and you haven't eaten yet. Come on down to the kitchen with us and at least have a sandwich."

"Mom…"

"Please."

Annie took her mom's advice, except she had soup instead of a sandwich. Then she went to bed and quickly fell asleep.

"I wish I could be of more help," Rhys said later, as they curled up together on the sofa. Summertime in Florida was no time for a fire in the fireplace, but gazing at the cool, dry logs provided its own kind of comfort. "Computer technology, when it gets more complicated than what I need to know, is unfortunately beyond me," he added.

"Just having you here is 'help' enough. You keep me from being as worried as I probably would have been; and you keep me from being lonely and scared. When I'm with you, I'm not afraid of anything, Rhys. Not even Forrest Fletcher."

"I can't imagine what kind of man would take pleasure in tormenting women."

"Right now, I think it's just me he's tormenting. Nineteen years ago there were other girls; but I was the one who turned him in, and he blames me for sending him to prison. It's true; I did."

"Which he soundly deserved. … You said he was a good citizen; I wonder what changed him."

"I'm not sure he ever was a good person, deep inside. I think it was all an act.

The man he portrayed to the public was a stage character—someone he created for his own selfish purposes. Dad said that Fletch's mother left his father and him when Fletch was a small boy. Mr. Fletcher never talked about it, but one of the neighbors said that Mrs. Fletcher was not happy being a farmer's wife and said she couldn't 'manage that child.' I gather Fletch had some unruly episodes early on."

"Maybe he couldn't help himself. Maybe he's—what's the word for it—schizophrenic?"

Susan shrugged and sighed. "I don't know what went wrong. Everyone in Davenport thought Fletch was a good man."

"Huh. A good man with a secret life."

Susan put her arms around Rhys and snuggled even closer. "I'm so glad you're here," she said, "and that we don't have secrets. I'm so glad you're *you*...that you're *still* you."

"I love you," he whispered. "Always have; always will."

Chapter 25

Beth phoned Susan the next morning, as early as she dared. "We really like your Welshman!" she said. "He's everything you said he'd be."

"And more." Susan glanced at Rhys on the other side of the bed and sighed, thinking about his kisses, his gentle touch, his lovemaking...

"Hey!" Beth broke into her thoughts. "Where'd you go?"

Susan laughed. "You know where, you old witch."

"Ain't love grand?"

"Grand, indeed, Sis. Hey, thanks again for meeting us at the airport the other night and for that wonderful meal."

"You're welcome. The meal was Marlena's choice. I think next time you and Rhys visit *I'll* cook. We'll have aphrodisiac cuisine—asparagus with almonds, oysters, and of course chocolate. We'll call it a love feast!"

"Oooo, I like the sound of that!...Beth, you're the greatest. I'm so glad you're my sister." She sighed. "Really glad, and I mean it."

"I know you do. I love you too. So how about dinner with us tomorrow night? Please say yes. And bring Annie too."

"Can't bring Annie without Brian."

"Oh boy. This love stuff is too much! I guess Marlena will want Max to be here too. See you then?"

"See you then."

Rhys rolled over, rubbing his eyes. "I gather that was Beth."

"Mmhmm. She likes you. Everyone does."

"I like your family, too, sweetheart. So when do I get to meet Brian? Anwen seems quite serious about him."

"Tomorrow night. Dinner at Beth's; he'll be there. You would have met him sooner, but Brian is carrying a full load at the university, plus working in the library; and now he's helping Annie track Fletcher's e-mail. I don't know him very well yet myself, but I do like what I've seen so far. He's absolutely devoted to Annie."

"That's understandable. She's a lot like her mother. . . . And I'm absolutely devoted to her mother."

~　~　~

Just after lunch, Annie had a breakthrough in her search for "Beethoven." Her hours of meticulous sleuthing, following traces that Fletcher thought were hidden, had finally paid off. Plus, Brian had positively identified Fletcher as the obnoxious "Dusty" of the chat rooms. Forrest Fletcher was smart, but in his haste he had been a wee bit careless. The proxy server he'd chosen was one of many that bent the code of ethics and recorded its users' information, including unencrypted logins and passwords. Moreover, a chain of proxies had been set up, ostensibly to hide information, but actually leaving a data trail along the chain. Brian had been right: Fletcher was operating under a false sense of security.

Annie, in her excitement, tried to explain it to Susan.

"You're speaking a foreign language, Annie! I don't understand a word of it."

"How about this: We got him!"

". . . You're serious?"

"Never more so. It's all right here." She tapped at the papers in her hand. "This is as good as a fingerprint."

Susan was nearly speechless. She gave her daughter a big, grateful hug. "What's our next step?" she asked.

"We call Grandpa and e-mail everything I found to his law office."

"Annie, you're wonderful."

"I'm not wonderful, but I am a fast worker. There's no telling how long we'd have waited for someone at the GBI to do this. It certainly wouldn't have been their first priority. This way, the detective work is done. All they have to do is verify it and arrest the bastard."

"Well, it's still early enough in the day that Dad should be able to get some action," Susan said. "I'll call him now; you send the e-mail."

Annie turned back to her PC. "That creep Fletch—*Lech*—has broken the law again and he needs to pay for it big time!"

~　~　~

Susan is going to pay for what she did to me. She's going to pay big. And soon! Forrest

Fletcher was seething. Each day it got worse. There were voices in his head, reminding him that he was a good person. He'd always been good—a good boy, a good son. Everything bad that had ever happened to him had been someone else's fault. Ernie Pelk had made him set fire to that cat when they were little kids. Fortunately, only his dad found out and they buried the cat. That was Ernie's fault. And if that dumb Matt Plummer had got out of Fletch's way when all the kids were walking to the ball field that day, Fletch wouldn't have had to break his leg with a baseball bat. That was Matt's own dumb fault! *Dumber Plummer!* Dad paid the doc, though, and gave Matt's mom some extra money too. Pops was the only one who ever understood. *He protected me from everyone who picked on me. Well, until Susan Evans sent me to prison. Never heard from him again. . . . But I'd made him proud for a lot of years. He hadn't known about my little hobby with the young girls. Wasn't any reason for him to know. Probably wouldn't have been too happy about it, but he would've understood. He was proud of me!*

Yes, Fletch was a good boy from a good family. Except for his no-good mother who ran off before she barely got to know him. She'd had no reason to run off. She was a grownup—she should've known how to take a joke. The snakes were just a joke! Fletch had always been a good little boy. . . . He rubbed his eyes. *Damn Susan Evans!* She had caused the biggest problem of all. He couldn't remember when he didn't hate her. The hate had started long before he went to prison, long before the night he finally controlled her, long before he asked her for that first date.

~ ~ ~

"I have an idea," Annie said to her mother. "Let's go to a movie tonight—you and Rhys and me. Some good ones are playing at Governor's Square. We can pick one we like and forget all about the Lech, at least for a while."

"Yes! I would love it. . . . Oh, but what about Brian? Don't you two have plans?"

"Not tonight. He has to work. But he has tomorrow off, and we're going to spend the whole day together. The mall, lunch at a special place—Brian won't tell me where—and an afternoon concert in the park."

"Don't forget you're both invited to Beth's for dinner tomorrow night."

Annie gave Susan a playful nudge. "How could I forget? Brian and Rhys—two Welshman—will meet for the first time. We wouldn't miss it!"

"Oh! I never told Rhys that Brian is Welsh."

"Then let it be a complete surprise. That should be fun! And, Mom—Brian and I are not coming back here between the concert in the park and going to Aunt Beth's tomorrow, so you and Rhys will have this house all to yourselves for a few hours."

"We'll behave."

"Hah!"

~ ~ ~

By two o'clock the next day, Friday, Susan still hadn't heard from her father about whether Fletcher would be arrested. So she called him.

"Nothing yet, honey," Tom said. "Only that they're working on it. You know how they have to double-, triple-, and quadruple-check every detail before taking action. I'll let you know as soon as I hear something."

"I'll be at Beth's tonight. You can call me there."

"Will do."

Going to the movie with Annie and Rhys the night before had been a great stress-reliever, at least temporarily. *Well,* she thought, *Forrest Fletcher and his problems are out of my hands.* She had done all she could; Annie had done her part; now it was up to the law.

For dinner at Beth's house, Susan chose a blue floral V-neck dress with a flirty hi-lo hem, knowing she looked good in it. She wanted Rhys to see her in something pretty, something other than the comfortable jeans and shirts she'd worn for the last three days and the back-packed travel clothes she'd worn in London. As she approached the front door, where he waited for her, the look on his face told her she'd chosen well. He lifted her off her feet and twirled her around.

Susan buried her face in his neck and giggled. "I feel like a teenager again," she said, "and it's a wonderful feeling!"

~ ~ ~

"Well, everyone's here but the lovebirds. Should I call Susan's cell phone?" Joel asked of no one in particular.

Beth and Anwen exchanged glances. "No, honey," Beth replied. "Give them a few more minutes. The potatoes aren't quite ready yet anyway."

The two young couples settled into one corner of the den. Annie had known Marlena's boyfriend, Max, since they were children. Both Marlena and Max were students at FSU but had never really met Brian, though they'd seen him in the library. "He's so cute!" Marlena whispered to Annie as the guys discussed FSU football.

"I'm glad you like him, because he's going to be around for a long time, maybe forever," Annie said.

Marlena's eyes grew wider. "You're that serious?"

Annie grinned. "I am. We are."

"They're here!" Beth called from the kitchen. "I heard a car in the driveway."

Everyone ran to the front door, and Beth jerked it open before Susan could ring the bell. "Come in! Come in!" she cried, staring at Rhys. "He still looks like Pierce Brosnan to me," she said to Susan in a stage whisper that everyone heard. Laughter erupted, and Susan shoved Rhys inside where he was welcomed by Joel and Marlena and introduced to Max. The last one to shake his hand was Brian, who introduced himself: "Brian Gruffydd," he said. "I know you'll like Tallahassee—and this wonderful family—as much as I do."

Rhys's ears perked up. "Brian Gruffydd. I detect a familiar accent. *Ach Cymraeg?* Are you Welsh?"

"*Do, chan Abertawe.* Yes, from Swansea," Brian replied.

Susan laughed. "Surprise!" She put her arm around Rhys's waist. "If it hadn't been for Brian," she said, "I wouldn't have found you. He's the one who translated those Welsh newspaper articles and sent Annie and me on our trek across Wales."

Rhys grabbed Brian's hand one more time, enclosing it in both of his. "*Diolch yn fawr*, my friend. Thank you very much! *Rwyt ti wedi achub fy mywyd.* You have saved my life."

Joel put steaks on the grill, and the new extended family spent the next two hours enjoying good food and one another's company. A sudden ring of the telephone interrupted the festivity.

Joel picked up the receiver, listened for a few minutes, then broke the news to the family. "That was Tom," he said. "Annie's research was right on target. They're going after Fletcher but of course won't say when. Could be tonight, tomorrow, the next day—whenever the opportunity is right. Fletch missed an appointment with his parole officer this afternoon, which adds to his troubles."

"Well, I certainly hope they get him soon," Beth said. "Susan has spent enough time worrying about what he might do. I still can't understand how anyone who seemed to be such a good member of the community could be so bad underneath."

"That's the problem—it was all for show. All of it."

After a few more hours of lively conversation, it was late, and Susan suggested to Brian that he spend the night at the home she shared with Annie. "Rhys will be there too," she said. "Annie and I have our own rooms, plus we have two guest rooms," she added with a wink.

Actually, Brian did choose a guest room. "Our first time…under your mother's roof?" he whispered as he kissed Anwen goodnight outside her bedroom door. "I don't think so." He smiled and added, "*Rwy'n dy garu di*, Anwen. I love you!"

Outside Susan's bedroom door, Rhys pulled her warm body close against his. "*Rwy'n dy garu di*, Susan."

She melted into his embrace, kissing him, feeling his breath merging with her own. "I love you too, Rhys," she whispered. "Very much."

Chapter 26

The voices in Forrest Fletcher's head were getting bolder, telling him what to do. All those years ago they told him he must do whatever it took to become an important person, and he obeyed them. He had dressed well, smiled; he shook hands, even though he knew the whole scene was crap. But he never had to pretend he was smart, because he was smart. Very smart. After he went to prison, though, the voices just whispered to him occasionally; they didn't protect him like he thought they should. But they did tell him that he had to get even with Susan Evans when he got out of prison, that everything was her fault. They just hadn't told him *how* to get even.

Now the instructions were more specific: *You need to go see her, Fletch. It doesn't matter that you're not permitted. You can watch her when she doesn't know she's being watched, then you can bump into her and pretend it was accidental, look into her eyes, give her a big grin and walk away. Scare the hell out of her! If she reports you, just say the meeting was accidental; you know you can talk your way out of anything.*

So he had an idea. He knew where she lived, in that hoity-toity section of Tallahassee. *Tomorrow is Saturday,* he told himself. *She'll be going out somewhere...and I'll be there. I'll get there early in the morning, before dawn, and park near her house, where I can see her leave. While it's still dark, maybe I'll peek in a window or two! Peek-a-boo! Ha! Ha!*

He might have a long wait. But that wouldn't matter. He'd pack a couple of sandwiches, some coffee, and a beer—ultra light, because he didn't want to get drunk and botch the fun. ...Actually, he did have a long wait, several hours.

~ ~ ~

Fletcher drove his father's car to Tallahassee in the wee hours of the morning. Finding Susan's house in the dark wasn't easy, even with the map he'd printed from Google. Too damned many winding, twisting streets. Finally, he located Susan's house and parked two doors away on the opposite side of the street, where he'd have a good view. At dawn the paperboy came riding along on his bicycle, tossing morning papers onto the lawns, and Fletch hunkered down in his seat so the boy wouldn't see him. Hours went by. Now it was mid-morning and he was getting antsy. He swallowed the last bite of his sandwich, hoping they'd hurry the hell up. He shifted in his seat. His back was starting to ache and he began to sweat. He hated the stink of his own sweat. *How much longer?*

Just then the front door opened and Susan came out to pick up the newspaper. *Wait… No! It's not Susan. Susan is older now. That girl looks just like Susan used to look.* She bent over to retrieve the paper, and her long blond hair fell forward over her shoulders. Fletch suddenly felt something strange inside his body, a kind of warmth that started in his head and settled somewhere north of his stomach. *It must be… It's… It's Annie.*

He watched the girl walk back to the door and disappear into the house. For a long time he didn't move. His eyes were vacant and his mind blank. Then, one big tear rolled down his cheek.

~ ~ ~

At Susan's house, everyone slept late on Saturday morning, so she laid out a simple brunch, continental-style. Eventually, the four of them gathered at the umbrella table on the back deck, each with a cup of coffee. The breeze was warm, and sun twinkled through the leaves of the huge magnolia tree in the back yard. If ever there were four happier people in one place at the same time, Susan could not imagine it. She thought Annie was absolutely glowing; and Annie said she had never seen her mother look more beautiful. As for the guys, well… *Guys don't exactly "glow,"* Susan thought, *but Rhys and Brian sure look happy.*

"So when's the wedding?" Annie asked.

Rhys laughed. "We've hardly had time to plan a wedding, Anwen." He pronounced her name *Anoowen*, as Brian did. Annie loved the sound of it.

"But you'll be the first to know," her mother said. "Will you be my maid of honor?"

Annie squealed. "Of course!" She lifted her coffee mug. "Cheers to the bride and groom who found each other after twenty-one years!"

"*Iechyd da!*" Rhys and Brian proclaimed in unison.

"Yacky dah? What's that?"

Brian laughed. "Cheers, of course. Good health. And now may I offer a blessing for the happy couple?" He raised his mug. "*Yn deisyf 'ch D llonaid chan des, Brydiau llonaid chan llonna, Cara a—*"

"Brian! Mom and I don't understand a word of it!"

Rhys offered the translation: "Wishing you—us—a house full of sunshine, hearts full of cheer, love that grows deeper each day of the year."

"*Gadael hi bod!* Let it be!" Brian finished.

"Let it be!" echoed Anwen and Susan.

Just then the mail carrier's vehicle appeared in the driveway at the back of the house. The elderly Mr. Grady climbed out and toted a bundle of mail up the steps of the deck. "Too much for the mailbox," he said, "and with all the noise back here, I figured you young folks were out and about." He put the mail on the table, and Susan introduced him to her guests.

"Mom and Rhys just got engaged," Annie said. "We were toasting them."

"Ah, in that case," he looked at Susan and Rhys, "allow me." He lifted his hand in the air. "This one's from me dear old Irish grandmother: 'May the road rise to meet you; may the wind be always at your back; may the warm rays of sun fall upon your home; and may the hand of a friend always be near.' God bless you, children," he added, waving as he drove off.

"It's not exactly like the Irish blessing I learned from Mrs. O'Neal next door," Annie said, "but it's close. More fitting, actually."

Susan quickly flipped through the envelopes, setting all but one aside. "Speaking of Irish," she said. "This envelope has a little shamrock sticker on the back of it."

"Who's it from?"

"I have no idea." Susan opened the envelope, removing one folded sheet of lined paper. She spread it out on the table. "Looks like a child's writing," she said.

"Probably a fan letter," Annie said, turning to Rhys. "Mom has quite a following, even among children. She sometimes takes her guitar to their schools and plays for them. They love her."

"I can understand that," Rhys said, smiling at his one true love.

"Read it to us, Mom."

Susan picked up the paper and began to read aloud:

> *Dear Ms. Evans,*
>
> *Robin gave me your CD, "Music of Many Lands," and I have listened to it over and over! My favorite song is "Carrickfergus" and you play it very beautiful! I saw your picture, too, and you are beautiful. This is my picture. I have a harp.*

Susan paused. "I didn't see a picture." She picked up the envelope and looked inside, pulling out a snapshot of a beautiful young woman sitting at a harp, her fingers on the strings. "But this isn't a child," she said. "It's a woman."

"Keep reading, Mom."

"All right." Susan picked up the letter once again:

> *Greg gave me the harp and it's almost like the one I have back home in Ireland. That's why I like to hear you play "Carrickfergus," because it's an Irish song. Of course it sounds different on my harp. I'm here for the winter now, staying with my sister and her husband at Haviland Plantation in Monticello, but I'll go back to Ireland in a few months. Robin says we're not far from Tallahassee. Maybe I can meet you sometime. But maybe you wouldn't want to meet me. I'm not famous like you. Anyway, I wanted to tell you how much I like your music.*
>
> *Love,*
> *Wrenny Riley*

"I'm confused," Susan said. "She writes like a child, but she's definitely a woman. Look." She passed the picture around the table.

"She could be an innocent," Brian offered.

"She's innocent? What do you mean?"

"Not *is* innocent. *An* innocent. It's what the Irish, and many of my own countrymen, call those whose minds aren't…well, fully developed."

"You see," Rhys injected, "she could be very bright, just not equal to her physical age. Like maybe she's thirty or so, but mentally like a ten-year-old who makes good grades in school."

"I am definitely going to answer her letter. Look at her—she's beautiful!" Susan tapped on the picture. "And that harp is not a toy; it's the real thing."

"Any mail for me, Mom?" Annie asked.

"Just junk." Susan pushed the pile into the middle of the table.

"What's this?" Annie lifted a small envelope that had been stuck between two gift catalogs. "It's for you, Mom. No return address."

Susan opened it and pulled out a single sheet. On it was a crude drawing of a "happy face," except the mouth had teeth. Beneath the drawing was written, "Peek-a-boo!" Susan's face took on a look of disgust, and she tossed the paper onto the table.

"What is it, love?" Rhys asked.

"More harassment. It's meaningless."

Brian picked up the envelope. "No return address, but it was postmarked in Albany on Thursday."

"Maybe it has fingerprints," Annie offered.

"You can be sure it does not," Susan replied. "He's smart. Remember? Just throw it away."

Annie picked it up with the junk mail, but she did not throw it away.

~   ~   ~

For the past hour Fletch still had not moved, except to slap that one big tear off his face. He'd slapped so hard he'd made his face sting. It was Susan's fault. *Everything is Susan's fault!* He rolled his window down to let the morning breeze in and took a deep breath. He knew there were people on Susan's back deck, because he could see part of the deck and some guy's elbow—*wonder who that might be.* And now, with the window down, he could hear laughter. Laughter! *She won't be laughing when I get through with her.*

Then the mailman came and went, and in a few minutes Fletcher saw the elbow guy stand up and knew they were going back inside the house. About time! He hoped the "peek-a-boo" picture he'd so carefully drawn had been in today's mailbag. Maybe that was what got sassy Susan off her sorry ass. *Hah! Sassy Susan's sorry ass!* He couldn't help admiring his clever use of words. *Sassy Susan's sorry ass!* He was getting excited; maybe he wouldn't have long to wait now. He'd had plenty of time to plan. He'd even looked in the rear-view mirror and practiced making some scary faces. Shit, one was so weird he'd almost scared himself! Couldn't wait to try that one on Sassy Susan. Or was it Sorry Susan? *She'll be sorry all right!* He looked in the mirror and made another face.

~   ~   ~

A few minutes later the foursome separated—Anwen and Brian to the university, and Susan and Rhys to the mall. They didn't notice the older model Buick pull away from the curb and follow Susan's car.

Going to the mall had been Rhys's suggestion. "I know you're anxious to hear from your father," he'd said, "but you can't just sit here waiting. Grab your cell phone in case he calls, and let's go shopping. Maybe I can find you a wedding present."

Susan's eyes lit up. "Maybe I can find one for you!"

Saturday-afternoon shoppers were plentiful, but Susan and Rhys didn't mind joining the crowd. The mall was two-storied in the shape of a cross, each wing with a variety of interesting shops, and Rhys headed straight for a jewelry store.

"Rhys!" Susan protested. "I have my engagement ring. I don't want what you call a 'proper' one. The one I have is special!"

"Who said anything about an engagement ring? I'm buying you a wedding present, so start looking." His smile was enchanting as he drew Susan toward a case of necklaces. "We need to replace your locket," he said. Absently, she reached up and rubbed her fingers across it. "The one you're wearing held a dream," he continued, softly. "But now the dream is reality. You need to wear something that gives you that assurance."

She wanted to hug him, kiss him, and hold tightly to him, right there in the store, but there were too many people close by. Instead, she concentrated on the jewelry case, tears in her eyes and a smile on her face. She tried on several necklaces, all beautiful, but could not make up her mind, so Rhys suggested they look in another store. "Take your time, love. After all, you're replacing something that's meant a lot to you over the years."

As they left the store, Susan noticed a man in the crowded walkway who was not walking but simply standing and staring. . .at her. Or so she thought. *Couldn't be me.* She turned around, but there was no one behind her. Rhys, not noticing, took her arm and moved her along toward another jewelry store in the next wing. This time, as she tried on necklaces, she noticed the same man staring at her through the window. The look on his face made her uncomfortable. She did not know him. The clothes on his thin frame were beyond casual, his hair rather unruly, and his face had a lot more beard than what her father would have called "five-o-clock shadow." *What is his problem?* she wondered.

Then she picked up the most beautiful necklace she'd ever seen. It was an emerald—her favorite stone—surrounded by eight diamonds, on a fine gold chain. She put it on and turned to face Rhys. Her smile told him that this was the one. "Perfect," he said. "You make the necklace look beautiful."

She laughed. "It's supposed to be the other way around—the necklace makes me look beautiful!"

As Rhys made the purchase, Susan glanced out the window, but the strange man was no longer there. They went to more stores, looking for a present for Rhys. Then, as they left a large department store and reentered the walkway, the man was suddenly in front of them. He looked at Susan and his mouth formed a wide, phony smile, showing lots of teeth. Abruptly, he turned and walked the other way.

"What was that all about?" Rhys asked.

"I…I have no idea. Just some weirdo, I guess." Actually, this time she did have an idea, and it gave her the creeps. The eyes were horribly familiar. He was much thinner, with more hair than he'd had years ago, and the ugly beginnings of a beard and bad grooming had made him unrecognizable. Almost. *Forrest Fletcher!*

"I'd like to use the restroom," she said to Rhys, needing some recovery time. "It's right here. I'll only be a minute."

"And I'll be in the store right across the way," he said. "Don't lose me—I'd never find my way back to your house!"

"I'm never going to lose you," she said, giving him a quick kiss, not caring who saw it. "It took me too long to find you!"

She took her time in the restroom, reapplying her lipstick, combing her hair…and thinking. Finally, she left and reentered the walkway, knowing how she would react if Fletcher showed his face again. Her reaction would be…*no* reaction. *Let's see how you like that, Mr. Forrest Fletcher who loves attention!*

As she turned and started toward the store where Rhys would be, Fletcher appeared again, right in her face. His mouth widened into the same ugly, phony smile. Then he said, "Peek-a-boo!"

Susan stood very still, staring at him as people shoved past them. She didn't say a word, just stared. Inside, she felt very tall and strong. And silently, to herself, she repeated her mantra several times, *Forrest Fletcher Is Finished!*

After what seemed like a long time but was probably less than a minute, Fletcher turned on his heel and stomped away, elbowing people as he pushed toward one of the mall exits. Shoppers were bewildered and indignant, some giggled and pointed at him, and Susan melted into the crowd that watched him disappear.

I did it, she thought. *I stood up to the bastard and I won!*

She hurried into the store across the walkway and found Rhys wandering the aisles. "Find anything interesting?" she asked. She would not tell him about Fletcher's staged appearance. She would not let Forrest Fletcher spoil their day.

"No, just browsing," Rhys answered.

"Getting tired?"

"Umhmm. And hungry. Let's go somewhere quiet, away from the crowds, and have an early dinner. Then…"

"Then?"

"Then go home and..."
"Go home and?"
He winked at her, and Susan knew exactly what he meant.

Chapter 27

The next morning Rhys and Susan drove to Davenport for Sunday dinner with Tom and Charlotte Evans. Charlotte had prepared her personal favorite—chicken divan with wild rice—and Rhys enjoyed it immensely. The table conversation moved easily from the weather to their evening at Beth's, to their day at the mall. Then, as before, it drifted toward England, Wales, and Rhys—a.k.a. David Lewellen. This time, Rhys modestly and unobtrusively chose to refocus it.

"I confess that I followed Susan's career for the last several years," Rhys said, "once I found her, that is, in magazines and on the Internet. Of course I've had her CD since it was released last year, and I've played it over and over. So beautiful." He glanced at his love. "But I guess I was a bit apprehensive about contacting her. She's famous," he whispered, with a wink and a smile.

"Not famous!" Susan said.

"*Almost* famous," her mother corrected.

"Fame is not what it's about. I do what I do because I enjoy it. I have loved playing the guitar ever since I first held one in my hands as a child."

"Yes, it was a present from your Uncle Fred, God rest his soul; and I will never forget when you played 'America the Beautiful' for our local Veteran's Day celebration. You were only twelve years old!" Charlotte said proudly. "And the very next year you won the state talent competition." Charlotte turned to Rhys. "The prize was a trip to Hawaii for four, so the whole family went—Susan, Beth, Tom and me!"

"Hmmm," Tom said. He was not smiling.

"Hmmm, what?"

"There was a little problem after that competition, something I never told you about, Charlotte; nor you, Susan."

"Problem?"

He nodded. "Later, I wondered if it might have had something to do with Fletcher's, uh, behavior toward you, Susan, when you were older."

"Fletcher? How does he figure in?"

"He, too, was a contestant in that talent competition."

Charlotte was suddenly alert. "Yes, he was! I remember now. He played...he played a guitar solo!"

"Very well, too. Not classical like you play, Susan. More country-style with fancy finger work. He was around twenty-one, twenty-two years old, and you were only thirteen." Tom looked at his daughter. "Fletcher didn't take the loss well at all. He stormed out of there complaining that the judges had chosen 'that brat' just because she was a kid, not because she played better than he did. After that, he started crop-dusting, built a lucrative business and became a model citizen, probably due to his father's influence. Harold Fletcher was a good man who worked hard and would have been embarrassed by such an outburst." Tom took a sip of his coffee. "I don't believe Forrest Fletcher ever played the guitar again. At least not in public."

Susan was stunned. "You mean...you think he chose me, specifically, to...to *rape?*"

"Oh, Tom," Charlotte said. "That can't be so."

He sighed. "I've considered it over the years. We all know the boy was brilliant. He wouldn't have forgotten a defeat like that. Maybe he didn't exactly plan it, but when Susan performed her senior recital at Theresa Malone's home, and he was one of the invited guests, the opportunity to meet 'the brat' as an adult—and get his revenge—was just too much of a temptation. That's what I think. I'm just damn sorry I didn't recognize it at the time. Like everyone else in this town, I was gullible. I bought into his 'good citizen' performance. He had no record. There was no indication that he was abusing young women—girls!" Tom reached across the table and patted his daughter's hand. His eyes were misty. "Forgive me, sweetheart."

"Dad, there's nothing to forgive. All you saw was one childish reaction years before. No one realized how volatile he could be. He never showed that side of himself in public. He was very good at concealing it. And he avoided sexual-abuse charges by threatening the girls, making them afraid of him. To all outward appearances, he was a model citizen. He really was."

"Was. That's a good word," Charlotte said. "I should feel guilty for saying it, but I'm glad he's a has-been, and I'm glad he went to prison. I just wish he could have stayed there!" She stood and pushed her chair back from the table. "Shall we adjourn to the parlor and plan a wedding?"

~   ~   ~

The weather that Sunday afternoon was beautiful, but Forrest Fletcher was in a foul mood. Again. Yesterday's face-to-face in the mall with Susan didn't elicit the response he'd been hoping for. He'd wanted to scare her, but the bitch just stood there staring at him. Oh yes, she recognized him all right. He could see it in her eyes. So why didn't she scream? He'd wanted her to scream or cry or something before he disappeared into the crowd. Anything! Not just stand there! He had looked, grinned, and said Peek-a-Boo, and…nothing. Not even a damned blink!

Right now he didn't care if he ever looked, grinned or play-acted again; he wanted to grab that holy-righteous whore and knock her around. She'd humiliated him in front of all those people! She was the one who should have been humiliated. People should have given her the same dirty looks they gave him. Didn't they see her kissing that pansy guy in public, right in the mall? *Probably kisses everyone who wears pants, yet in court she'd called me, Forrest Fletcher, a pervert! I won't forget that!* He'd like to take that fancy guitar of hers and smash it over her head, just like he'd smashed his own guitar over a fence post more than twenty years ago. That would be real payback! Suddenly, he burst into tears…and that in itself made him even angrier—he was a *man*; he shouldn't be crying like a damned woman! What was the matter with him lately? *Tears?* Had Susan Evans turned him into a sissy?

Forget about her, Fletch! the voice in his head called to him. *Go have some fun!* said another one. They didn't have to tell him twice. He grabbed his gear, picked up a couple of cans of beer, and headed for his plane. He would fly up and down and around, and over and under, scare some birds, and have a good time! He deserved a good time!

Within minutes he was in the air, playing with his crop-duster as if it were a toy. He flew high over the trees and low under the electrical wires, sometimes one-handed, enjoying his freedom and his beer. Then he left his property and buzzed the mom & pop gas station at the crossroads. Old Pop Higgins came out and shook his fists in the air. Fletcher laughed and dipped his wings. That was fun. The farmer in the next field was walking through his rows of corn, checking the ears, so Fletch flew low enough over him to make the man duck. That was double fun! Then he headed toward town; and, after several more maneuvers he thought were downright dazzling—must have been dazzling because cars were stopping in the streets and people were coming out of their houses to watch him—he circled around and flew back toward his own property.

As he approached, he saw a police car creeping down the lane toward the house. *Are they coming to complain about my flying? Did that chicken-shit farmer call them? Did those wimpy townfolk tattle on me? …Oh, damn! I missed the appointment with my P.O. yesterday. That's it. Why do they even care?*

He flew around back toward the hangar, staying high in the air. It was then he spotted more police cars—one sitting on the side of the highway and two in the back, tucked under the trees. *Why so many cars just to give me a warning? …Or is it something else? Did Susan Evans call them? But they can't know it was me who e-mailed her. I made sure of it! And she could never prove I was in the mall yesterday. Must be my flying. Hell! I was just having some fun.*

The car that had entered the lane pulled up to the hangar and stopped. The cop got out and looked up at the sky. Fletch took another swig of his beer and felt his heart begin to race. *He knows it's me up here. Does he think I'm going to come down now, with all his buddies nearby?* A moment of panic. What should he do? Then the voices started telling him: *This is your show, Fletch. You're in the pilot's seat. Don't let them intimidate you. Don't let them take you back to prison on some trumped-up charge. Just fly away. Fly away to some place where they'll never find you. But first…first have some fun with the sons of bitches!*

So he did. He buzzed the treetops over the two police cars concealed beneath the branches, then turned and flew low toward the deputy who was standing near the hangar, pulling the nose of the plane up at the last second. The officer had flattened himself on the ground, and Fletcher laughed and laughed. He circled around again. By this time, the officer was back in his car and all four cars were moving out into the open. *What the hell do they think they're doing? Going to shoot my powerful machine down with their little guns?* He laughed again. *No one can fly a plane like I can! I'll give them a show they'll never forget!*

He flapped his wings, turned the plane over and flew upside down in circles, righted it, then tried some maneuvers he hadn't even thought about since getting out of prison. It was obvious to those on the ground that his control was out of sync. The maneuvers were wobbly, even scary, but Fletcher didn't notice. He only knew that he was invincible.

Do it, Fletch, the voices urged. *Show them your stuff!* Fletcher felt better than he had in days. He could do anything! He could even park this baby in the hangar without slowing down. "Watch this!" he yelled into the roar of the engine, unheard by anyone other than himself. "Watch close, you wimps! You'll never see anyone do this again!"

~   ~   ~

That afternoon, as Fletcher showed the world what he could do with an airplane, Tom, Charlotte, Susan and Rhys sat in Charlotte's slightly uncomfortable "parlor" making wedding plans. Tom would have preferred the TV room, but he loved his wife and often indulged her Victorian fantasies. Actually, the new little family group talked more than they planned; however, they did choose a tentative date in early October, which would depend on the availability of the church.

"It's a lovely place," Charlotte had suggested, "a small Anglican church in the countryside not too far from Tallahassee. Tom and I went to a wedding there just last summer."

"Anglican? I'll feel right at home," Rhys said with a warm smile.

"Who will be your maid of honor?" Charlotte asked her daughter.

"Annie has already consented."

"Perfect!"

"And I'm hoping Brian will be my best man," Rhys said. "I'd feel very comfortable with a fellow Welshman. Besides, I really like him."

The preliminary guest list was short: Tom and Charlotte Evans; Beth and Joel Montgomery; Marlena and her boyfriend, Max. And from London—Brisen, Kent, and Nia. In addition, some of Susan's friends from the university would be invited. There would be others, of course.

One issue was deciding where they would live after they were married, but for Susan it was not a problem. She wanted to join Rhys in London.

"I can teach or perform anywhere, Rhys," she'd said. "Your business is there, and you can't move it. Besides, I love London; you know that."

"Just so you love me," he replied, not one bit embarrassed to say it in front of Susan's parents.

"Always have; always will. By the way, I have an idea for our honeymoon."

"Uh-oh. Something exotic? Maybe Tasmania? Or cold and wild, like Iceland?"

"No." She smiled. "I think we should go to Wales. Visit Trefriw, Llandudno, Bodnant Garden, and other places we saw together as teenagers."

"What a delightful idea!" Charlotte cried.

Rhys was hesitant. "The prodigal son returns?"

"Yes. Rhys, everywhere Annie and I went in Wales, people spoke lovingly of you. Not one had a bad word to say. I'm sure they would like to see you again and know that you are successful and happy."

"Hmmm." He pretended to consider. "Could we stay at the Clarence Hotel and sneak out to the car park at night and kiss?"

Susan laughed. "Just like we used to."

"Susan, you did that?" her mother asked, bright-eyed. Tom gave a hearty chuckle.

"Yes, Mom. And we must do it again. The trip wouldn't be complete without it!"

Just then the phone rang, and Tom went to the kitchen to answer it. In a few moments he returned. "You'll have no more trouble from Forrest Fletcher," he said.

"Oooh, thank you!" Susan said, with a sigh of relief. "They caught him, then? He'll be going back to prison?"

"Not exactly." Tom relayed what had happened, that the officers had approached the Fletcher farm cautiously, expecting trouble. "They thought he might be difficult, because he'd been flying his plane dangerously close to people and buildings, like he was mentally or emotionally out of control."

"Of course he was—*is*—out of control. He always has been!"

"Well, Fletcher spotted the police and decided to show off like some barnstorming daredevil. I can't imagine his reasoning, if he 'reasoned' at all. It's like he suddenly had a death wish, putting his plane through dangerous acrobatics when he hadn't done that kind of thing for years. Hell, he'd been in prison for nineteen years and only out a couple of weeks. It's not like he'd had time to practice!"

"So what happened?"

"His last trick was to fly his plane into the hangar."

"*Fly* it in?"

"Yes. He flew it into that wide-mouth door…and right through the back wall. It nosed into the ground and burst into flames."

"Is he…?"

"He's dead."

~   ~   ~

The relief Susan felt over Forrest Fletcher's death was nearly palpable. As Rhys drove Susan back to Tallahassee, she lay her head back against the headrest and closed her eyes. Her biggest fear—that somehow Forrest Fletcher would harm Annie—was resolved. He could no longer worm his way into their lives. She had been right to be afraid of him. All those years in prison did not make him sorry for what he had done to those girls, to her, and did not make him a better man. He was sick. She didn't know if he had been schizophrenic or a sociopath or a psychopath—he was sick. And it didn't matter any more.

"Are you all right?" Rhys asked quietly.

She opened her eyes and turned her head to face him. "Oh yes," she said with a sigh. "I'm fine, but…"

"But what?"

She sat up straight. "I feel guilty for being relieved that a man is dead. That doesn't seem right."

"It's the goodness inside of you that enables you to feel sorry for him," Rhys said. "I'm relieved, too, and I don't feel a bit sorry about it."

"But that doesn't make you a bad person."

He smiled. "No, just a different shade of good. I do believe in justice, and I'm thinking that Mr. Fletcher chose his own justice."

"He chose it?"

"Yes. For whatever reason, he *decided* to fly the plane into that hangar. It was his choice."

Susan gave it some thought. "…I can live with that," she said finally.

Postlude

Three months after Forrest Fletcher's demise, the pianist at the little Anglican church near Tallahassee, Florida, played the Wedding March for Susan and Rhys. Pre-ceremony music was beautifully presented on a harp by Wrenny Riley. Her music wasn't typical "wedding music." Rather, she played songs she knew—Irish songs, including "Londonderry Air" and her own favorite, "Carrickfergus." Susan was delighted. The beautiful sound reminded her of the Welsh harpist Rhys had introduced to her group so many years ago. Wrenny's sister and brother-in-law, Robin and Greg Haviland, had arranged for the harp to be delivered from Monticello, and they brought Wrenny to the wedding. "It's perfect!" Susan said after rehearsal on the previous night. "I am so glad I answered Wrenny's letter."

Susan and Rhys had found new friends in Robin and Greg and had spent some happy days at their plantation. "You can expect us to visit you in London," Robin had said to Susan. "Twice a year we go to Ireland, collect Wrenny and bring her here for a couple of months, then take her back; and, you know, London is just a short hop from Ireland!"

Susan walked down the aisle in an ankle-length, Victorian-style dress, which her mother had worn on her own wedding day forty years before. That was Susan's "something borrowed." Beth provided her with a lacy garter, "something blue." At her neck, was "something new"—the emerald and diamond necklace, her gift from Rhys. And, concealed beneath the folds of her bodice was "something old"—the locket, still holding the smiling young faces of Susan Evans and Rhys Llewellyn.

At the close of the wedding ceremony, the priest said, "Rhys and Susan, you are completing your lives. You are walking a path you started to walk many years ago but were unable to finish. This time the world awaits you—the two of you, together. . . . God bless you!"

At the reception Nia scooped her father and her new stepmother into a big three-way hug. "I am sooo happy for you both! This is like a wonderful fairy tale with the very best kind of ending!" Annie joined them, and Brisen, and Kent, and Tom, and Charlotte, and Beth, and Joel, and Marlena; and the new blended family began a circle dance—a perfect circle with no broken pieces. As they danced, Anwen blew a kiss to Brian outside the circle, hopeful that he would join the family when the time was right. He returned the kiss and added a wink.

One very special wedding gift stood out among the others. Actually, it was a joint gift from Annie and Nia. With Mrs. Newbury's help, Nia had "borrowed" the Great Orme photo from the house in High Wycombe, had made a copy, and returned it without her father's knowledge. Meantime, Annie had snapped a picture of Susan and Rhys at Haviland Plantation one beautiful sunny day, when they'd all visited Wrenny, Robin and Greg. Annie had intentionally positioned the lovebirds as they had been in the earlier photo— looking at each other, smiling brightly. Both photos had been arranged and matted into one large frame; and, beneath the pictures, Brisen had written in her beautiful calligraphy, "From long ago and far away, love brought us to our wedding day." That thoughtful gift took center stage on the gift table.

~　~　~

Honeymooning in Wales, Rhys and Susan received congratulations from old Mrs. Awbrey at Snowdonia Tours in Conwy, and from Mr. Cretney at the Clarence Hotel in Llandudno. And, yes, the honeymooners snuck out to the car park at night and kissed!

In Betws-y-Coed, old Mrs. Jervis was thrilled to see "that boy" she'd always cared for and worried about.

"I knew ye'd make good," she said to Rhys. "I had faith ye'd amount to more than just a general dogsbody."

"Dogsbody?" Susan asked.

"A gofer," Rhys explained, grinning.

Best of all was Rhys's return to the area around Arnhall Orphanage where he'd grown up. The orphanage was no longer there, but some of the "old boys" who'd bought him candy still hung around the pubs, and Rhys sought them out.

"Well now, young Rhys, did ye become a big important person out there wherever ye were?"

Rhys smiled and told a tiny lie: "No, just a simple tour guide. You fellows were right."

"We knew that then. Ye belong here, y'know, among yer people."

I am among my people, Rhys thought. *My Susan, my family…my people.*

~ ~ ~

Shortly after Susan and Rhys returned from their honeymoon, Annie received an unexpected letter from a law firm in Albany, Georgia. A handwritten will had been found among Forrest Fletcher's possessions. It was dated the day before he died and named Anwen Evans the sole heir to his estate, valued at $3.5 million.

Annie was stunned. "Why me?" she asked her mother. "I thought he hated us."

"I don't think he ever hated you, Annie. Just me. I'm sure he suspected you were his daughter. Maybe this was his way of making things right."

~ ~ ~

The following year, Susan Evans Lewellen performed as a guest soloist with the London Symphony. Her husband sat in the audience, listening proudly to his wife's rendition of "Rhapsody on a Theme of Paganini." And in his hands his fingers gently caressed the most precious of lucky charms—the locket.

Author's Notes & Acknowledgments

For those very sharp readers who are sticklers for detail, the settings in this book are as accurate as I could make them. I do admit to taking a few liberties with dates, and any errors—intentional or not—are entirely my own. This is a work of fiction, and all of the characters, locations, and events portrayed are either products of my imagination or are used fictitiously.

I would like to thank my son, Mark, for sharing his expertise in computer technology. Also, thanks to my "first readers" who provided invaluable comments and encouragement—Linda Fullerton, Betty Westley, and Diana Williams. And, a big thank you to my husband, Doug, for his love and support.

At the risk of seeming a bit unconventional, I would like to thank a fictional character, Wrenny Riley, for her contribution to this book. Wrenny first appeared in my novel, *Chain of Deception* (PublishAmerica 2005), where her story and that of her family came to light after years of secrecy. Wrenny, one of my favorite characters, begged me for another appearance!

Printed in the United States
208819BV00001B/80/P

9 781607 030294